WHERE'S LAURA?

A TUESDAY TABLE LADIES' MYSTERY

OCTAVIA LONG

ISBN: 978-1-63385-172-6
Library of Congress Control Number: 2016916312

Design and Layout by
Jason Price

Published by
Word Association Publishers
205 Fifth Avenue
Tarentum, Pennsylvania 15084

www.wordassociation.com
1.800.827.7903

Acknowledgments

This book could not have been written without the supportive climate of Longwood at Oakmont in western Pennsylvania. We were urged on by the kindly curiosity of our fellow residents. Our appreciation of the dining staff and the good food at Longwood is evident throughout the book.

We are especially grateful to the young man and his helpers who disposed of the endless amount of recyclable paper we generated.

Kevin Kramer, our computer guide, introduced us to the Dropbox so aptly designed for a collaborative project such as ours, and Mark Novaleski guided us to our publisher.

We benefited greatly from various how-to books and a publishing workshop at the Oakmont Mystery Lovers' Bookshop.

We also called upon and tested the patience of friends and family members (especially Marion and Sarah Golin and Martha Browne) whose professional knowledge and experience far exceeded ours.

All the faults in this book are ours, and we proudly claim them!

Could it be, even for elderly people,
that this was life?—
startling, unexpected, unknown?

—VIRGINIA WOOLF

Contents

Characters

RESIDENTS

Sandra Brown—*consultant in information science*

Barbara Jackson—*lawyer and homemaker*

Laura Lambert—*lawyer*

Ellen Moore—*high school math teacher*

Harriet Parker—*social worker*

Karen Taylor—*columnist*

Robert Symonds—*State Department officer*

OAKWOOD STAFF

Catherine Evans—*executive director*

Nora—*housekeeper*

Augusta—*housekeeper*

Emily—*dining room server*

Kevin—*dining room server*

Patti—*hairdresser*

OTHER

Steve O'Malley—*FBI agent*

Prologue

I t was a cool, brisk October morning when a tall, distinguished gentleman entered the hotel. Grateful for the warmth of the lobby, he reflected that perhaps he should have worn a topcoat. Robert hadn't realized that the temperature had dropped so quickly overnight. He knew Washington, DC, could be cool in the fall, but the day was unusually cold. He came every month for lunch with his former State Department colleagues.

Startled by a sudden tap on the shoulder, he turned to face a slightly shorter man with an athletic build who was smiling broadly.

"It really is you?" the man exclaimed. "After all these years to see you here. I cannot believe it!"

At first, Robert failed to respond to the friendly greeting. The face was vaguely familiar. But the accent was unmistakable. In a flash of memory, he realized who this man was. It seemed almost surreal to see him in the lobby of a hotel in the United States. *What's he doing here?* Robert wondered. He was uncomfortable and hesitated a moment before speaking. "You're the last person I expected to see. What brings you here?" Robert asked somewhat stiffly. He was uncomfortable. Their last meeting, years ago, had been difficult. *How can he be so pleased to see me?*

CHAPTER ONE

The Table

*We love to be with family and friends and I can
tell you lots of eating will be involved.*

—JULIA BARR

"I don't think we should wait any longer. I'm hungry." Sandra looked around her table at the four women seated there. "I wonder where Laura could be. She's never this late. Maybe she fell asleep."

"I'll call her apartment," Barbara said as she pulled her phone from her pocket. "Perhaps she just lost track of time."

"Yes, she might be playing FreeCell on her computer," Sandra said. "She's addicted to that game."

"No answer. I think we should go ahead and order," said Barbara. She motioned their young server over.

Emily, her long, dark hair pulled into a ponytail, was dressed in black pants and white shirt as were her fellow servers. She moved quickly to the table and noted the vacant chair. "Do you want to order now?"

"Yes. If she comes in late, you can take her order then," Sandra said. "What's tonight's special?"

As the women perused their menus, Emily recited a description of the special catch of the day and quickly jotted down their choices. She picked up the chilled Pinot Grigio Harriet had brought. She would open it in the kitchen and return with wine glasses.

Emily quickly returned and served the wine. The diners were waiting for their soups and salads, all of them looking at each other and wondering about Laura's absence.

The five well-dressed women were in their seventies and eighties with graying or white hair. They were typical of the residents at Oakwood Retirement Village—well educated and active retirees. Their fellow residents who had suffered serious illnesses or falls had moved on to one of the health care units; the women at the table were relatively healthy, independent, and engaged in the community as well as in the many activities at Oakwood.

Harriet Parker was sitting in her usual place—back against the wall. She surveyed the dining room with her piercing blue eyes. She was eighty-two. She sat erect, her back as straight as ever; she had lost little of her six feet. Even seated, she was an imposing figure. She would always arrive at dinner precisely five minutes before their reservation to ensure getting her particular seat, which gave her a view of the entire dining room whose tables were set for two, four, six, or eight guests. White table-cloths with colored napkins brightened the room and complemented the upholstered dining chairs.

As one of the longest residents at Oakwood, Harriet was always eager to greet new residents warmly. But she would follow that with relentless inquiry into their previous lives, the whereabouts of their children, and their current marital statuses. Though persistent in her questioning, she was so friendly and empathic that it was difficult for those undergoing her examination to take offense, so she was usually able to give her tablemates a summary of the newcomer's life story in short order.

She noted that Henry was eating with Martha for the third time that week and considered what that might mean. She had heard a rumor that Martha had been involved in some "unpleasantness" and wondered how she might find out more about it.

Karen Taylor pulled a slip of paper out of her pocket. "While we're waiting, I can give you my household hint for the day!" Seventy-nine-year-old Karen wore her usual outfit—a solid-color blouse and jacket with matching pants. Short and sturdy, she was always easy to spot as she walked around the campus with her military bearing, striking the ground decisively with her cane. Despite her severe demeanor, she was a caring person, and people quickly sensed she was much less formidable than she at first appeared.

In addition to her extensive and demanding volunteer work with a food bank and other organizations, Karen had always been a proud and meticulous homemaker full of wonderful tips about ways to make life easier and more pleasant around the house. For several years, she had shared her household hints in a weekly column that ran in the local newspaper. Though she no longer wrote her column, she still loved to share her ideas; the women at the Tuesday Table expected to hear a weekly household hint from Karen's seemingly endless supply whether they wanted to or not.

After Karen explained how to get rid of kitchen ants, Ellen and Barbara shared their experiences with stink bugs while Harriet surveyed the dining room. She saw Ed go to the men's table. She smiled as she recalled the recent start of that new Tuesday night innovation. About a month ago, Sandra had told her, "Well, it seems that some of the fellows have noticed how much fun we six gals have when we get together. They're so outnumbered by us women that they seem to have a hard time getting to know each other. Now, they've arranged to have a table set up every Tuesday night just for men, and up to eight of them can have dinner together without having to make reservations."

It had been a good idea. Several men were there each week. Harriet thought they should be more organized. She told Ellen, "Men never call each other to make proper arrangements. At the men's table, they come in at various times, and the poor servers are serving desserts to some and soup to others. Oh well, they seem happy. I've suggested to some of them that they might want to set a gathering time, but they'll probably never do that."

The women's Tuesday Table had evolved almost by accident. Harriet, who was the first of the group to move into Oakwood, had invited Ellen Moore and Barbara Jackson to join her for dinner shortly after they had arrived. They enjoyed each other's company so much that they soon found themselves getting together for dinner every Tuesday. And Karen Taylor and Sandra Brown were invited to join the table shortly after they moved in as well. Finally, Laura Lambert, the most recent arrival, was invited to join the group by Barbara, who had worked in a law firm with Laura many years before.

The women had moved to Oakwood after losing their husbands through death or divorce. They all wanted to maintain their independence but to stay close to their children and grandchildren. Oakwood was the perfect solution. Only Harriet had grown up in the area; the others had relocated there from elsewhere.

The other diners had noted the big smiles and the hearty laughter that consistently came from their table each Tuesday and had dubbed them the Tuesday Table Ladies. When they heard of this, the six women were amused and indeed embraced the title. Though there were other groups who ate together regularly, none seemed to have as much fun as those at the Tuesday Table, whose corner table in the Riverview dining room was always reserved for them on that day of the week.

The conversation was interrupted by soups and salads brought by Emily. "I do love their soups," said Harriet, "especially this pumpkin bisque." That evening's salad was a pear half with blue cheese and walnuts, but two of the group chose instead to go to the salad bar, where they could choose their own ingredients.

Sandra's eyes were dancing when she returned from the salad bar with a large plate of lettuce and raw vegetables. "Did you see who just came to the men's table? Robert Symonds!"

Some of the others looked over to see the new arrival at the table—a suave gentleman who had only recently moved to Oakwood. The women thought of him as always charming but somewhat enigmatic. Laura, who had known him previously, had invited him to join them for dinner one evening shortly after he arrived at Oakwood, and they all enjoyed the lively conversation that he sparked. Harriet of course had already noted his arrival in the dining room.

"Okay, ladies," said Ellen, bringing their attention back to the table, "I know he's an interesting guy, but I'm worried about Laura. It's quite unusual." Ellen was a retired high school math teacher. Small and slender with large, blue eyes that gave her a look of perpetual surprise, she had been at Oakwood almost ten years, having moved there to be near her eldest daughter. Despite a sometimes painful back, she was diligent in her exercise regime and equally driven by her computer. While her neighbors were playing FreeCell or doing Lumosity brain exercises, Ellen was googling and yahooing her way through a variety of subjects. As she had often remarked, "There's no information you can't discover if you know how to ask."

While they enjoyed their salads, Sandra complained, "Would you believe it? They were out of anchovies. I think someone took the whole plateful. It's not really a Caesar salad without anchovies."

Sandra was even more a computer geek than was Ellen. After escaping from a marriage to the wrong man, she had made a comfortable life for herself and her two children. She had earned an advanced degree in information science, established a consulting company, and still took on an occasional consulting assignment. Like the others, she had come there to be near her children. Oakwood was almost exactly equidistant between her son and daughter. Considered one of the most attractive of the Tuesday Table Ladies—second only to Laura—she looked much younger than her seventy-six years.

The conversation soon turned back to Laura's unexplained absence. As she poured a glass of wine and passed the bottle to her left, Barbara said, "I just don't understand it. She's never missed our Tuesday dinners without letting one of us know. In fact, she told me yesterday she was looking forward to dinner tonight."

They enjoyed their meal as well as the view of the sky taking on varying hues of gold, orange, and red. The dining room was called Riverview because it was perched on the banks of a wide river that slowly meandered to its mouth on the Chesapeake Bay. The floor-to-ceiling windows faced the water; that night, the sunset was particularly colorful. Though it was too cool to dine outside, their table was near the windows, and they enjoyed the view of the changing sky reflected in the water as well as the occasional sailboat making its way upriver to its berth at one of the many marinas on the river.

After Emily had served the various entrees— cranberry chicken for Ellen and Barbara, pecan-crusted trout for Harriet and Sandra, and beef burgundy for Karen—Barbara brought them back to the question of Laura's whereabouts.

"A long as I've known her, and we worked together in the law firm for several years, I never completely understood her, but she would never stand you up for lunch or a meeting, and she was always careful about showing up to her appointments on time. This just isn't like her. I'm starting to worry."

Barbara was known among her friends for her calm demeanor and air of quiet competence. Her professional practice had focused on family law; those characteristics were invaluable in helping women through painful divorces. She had occasionally worked with Laura on difficult cases, and they had become friends albeit not close. She was becoming increasingly concerned about her friend's absence.

"How did she get along at the office?" Sandra asked.

"She was very popular with the other lawyers and their wives," Barbara answered. "And she and Mike, her husband, entertained a lot, but sometimes in more-private moments, I sensed a pervasive, underlying sadness. Whenever I asked her if anything was wrong, she'd just shake her head and put on a big smile. I'm not sure what it meant, but I often wondered if it was because she and Mike had no children." Barbara was pensive. "She was really good with kids, and my three children *adored* her.

"She never said why they didn't have their own kids. Whether there was a medical problem or they just didn't want any, I don't know. They certainly had a very active social life while I was busy being a stay-at-home mom. After that, I saw Laura only sporadically for lunch or through mutual friends until she came here."

"Why don't you call her again?" Karen asked.

The women waited anxiously as Barbara dialed Laura's number.

"Still no answer. You heard me ask her to call when she got my message. I wonder if we should check her apartment."

"I hate to just look in someone's apartment, especially Laura's. She's so private about everything. I don't think she'd like it," Sandra said.

"Do you know if she locks her door?" asked Ellen.

"I don't think so," responded Barbara, who lived down the hall from Laura. "I usually stop by for her, but tonight, I came to dinner right from my bridge group, so I didn't call for her."

"Laura gave me a spare key so when she's away I can put a FedEx package inside her door or water her plants," Karen said. "But then, she always tells me when she's going to be away." Karen remembered one time Laura was away and her plants needed tending. In her diligence, Karen had overwatered the African violets and they developed root rot and had died. For someone who prided herself on her copious household hints, she felt she had fallen far short of her own expectations. With Laura's disappearance, she wondered if she might have missed something in the preceding days.

Harriet spoke. "Those of us in the cottages usually lock our doors because we're more isolated, but even in the apartments, it seems we should always lock our doors."

"They recommend that, but it's such a nuisance to carry keys around all the time. I often don't have pockets to put them in, so I just don't bother though I know I should," Barbara said.

Ellen patted her jacket pocket and made her keys jingle. "It's certainly safer for all of us if we keep our doors locked."

The others nodded.

By that time, the sky was a deep blue with orange and yellow streaks along the horizon. "It's getting dark so early now. Really depressing," Ellen said.

Emily took away their plates as they contemplated the dessert choices—carrot cake, apple pie, cappuccino crunch ice cream, or macadamia nut cookies.

Before she could give in to temptation, Ellen declared, "Just decaf for me."

"Me too," Karen said. "With nonfat milk please." She was thankful that skim milk no longer tasted like chalk. It was healthier than cream in her estimation.

The others were less restrained; they asked for apple pie, carrot cake, and ice cream along with two more decafs and a hot tea with lemon.

"I really think we should check out her apartment," Barbara said. "She could have passed out and be lying on the floor. No one would know until check-in tomorrow morning. That happened to a resident in one of the cottages." She shivered as she recalled the story her housekeeper had told her of stumbling across a resident's body when she arrived to clean the apartment.

Each unit had an electronic system that allowed residents to indicate they were okay by pressing a button every morning. Failure to check in would lead to a phone call and then a visit by Security to make sure there was no problem.

Prompted by the thought that at her age she might find herself in some difficulty, Ellen remarked, "I've often wondered how old Laura is. She's someone whose age is hard to pinpoint. I've always thought she was younger than us, but that might be because she has so much energy and is still so pretty."

"Maybe she ran off with someone's husband," Sandra said with a laugh.

"The way she flirts with all the men," added Karen mischievously.

"It's not really flirting," Ellen said. "It's just that she's so warm and attractive that men are naturally drawn to her, and women like her too."

"Come on now. Let's be serious. I'm worried," said Barbara, looking nervously around the table. "I think we should check on her."

"I think we should check with Security at the front desk and the health care center before we go barging into her apartment," Karen said. "Perhaps she felt ill and went to the health care center or was taken to the hospital."

"Let's go to the lobby after dessert and see if anyone else has seen her. We can check out the other dining room there as well as the desk. It's possible she forgot it's Tuesday and is eating with someone else in the Oak Hall dining room," Harriet said.

After dessert, the five women walked across the lawn to Oak Hall and into the lobby. Barbara approached the desk to ask about Laura and was told she had not signed out and no resident had gone to the hospital. A quick call to the health care center by the desk receptionist assured her that Laura was not there either.

The others checked out the dining room and the library with no success. They asked a couple of other residents, but no one had seen her.

"Hasn't she mentioned some place she used to go to occasionally?" Barbara asked.

"But then she would've signed out," Karen replied.

"Unless she forgot," Sandra said. "I've forgotten occasionally."

"This isn't getting us anywhere," Ellen said. "We need to go to her apartment, but maybe not all of us." She motioned to Barbara and Karen. "Why don't you two go? You live on her floor, so it's only natural you'd stop by."

"I'll stop at my place for her key," said Karen.

"Okay, we'll go," Barbara said, "but I think the rest of you should wait in the lobby. We'll be back in a few minutes."

Barbara and Karen walked down the connecting hallway to Laura's apartment building. The other three looked uneasily at each other. They were getting anxious. It wasn't like Laura.

It was dark outside. The lobby was eerily quiet. Most of the residents had returned to their apartments after dinner to watch TV or read. They were alone in the lobby. No lectures, music programs, or card games were scheduled for Tuesday nights. The three settled into large, comfortable chairs to wait.

"It's awfully quiet here," Ellen said, looking apprehensively around the lobby.

"You know, Laura has always been a bit of a mystery to me," Harriet said. "She manages to avoid any really personal questions, and she's evasive when questions about her background come up. I don't even know where she was born."

"I know that she's originally from around Boston and that she's been married a couple of times. I don't know why, but I have a feeling there might be a third marriage as well," Sandra said. "But you're right. She certainly never talks about her past. Most of us talk about our husbands once in a while if only to complain about them," she said with a smile. "But I don't even know who she was married to or for how long."

"Yes," Ellen said. "I've always thought of her as a mystery woman who seemed to be hiding something. She sometimes seemed sad despite her cheeriness. I figured it was none of my business, so I never pushed her. Besides, if you couldn't get anything out of her, Harriet, I don't think anyone could."

Harriet sat up straight and smiled.

"Actually, Barbara probably knows her better than anyone since they worked in the same law firm for so long," Sandra said, "but even she says she was never really close to Laura and doesn't know that much about her life before she joined the law firm. Apparently, she was a brilliant lawyer and made partner in the firm before she was thirty-five. The one thing we do know about Laura is that she's always let us know when she'd be away on Tuesday nights."

Their speculation was interrupted by a breathless Barbara who rushed up to them. "Come with me!" she demanded. "You need to see this. We don't know what to make of it!"

The three women quickly rose and followed her down the hall.

CHAPTER TWO

Laura's Apartment

The best thing to hold onto in life is each other.
—KATHERINE HEPBURN

B arbara refused to say anything else as they walked nervously to Laura's apartment, fearful of what they might find.

Karen greeted them excitedly at the door and hastily closed it behind them. "The door was locked, but I opened it with my key. Laura's not here and we have a couple of real mysteries!"

"Oh thank God she's not dead," Ellen said. "I thought maybe you'd found her body."

Barbara shook her head and led them into the kitchen of the spacious two-bedroom apartment. "Look at this paper we found on the island next to the phone. It's a copy of a work order Laura sent to the head of housekeeping. It's dated yesterday."

The women gathered round as Barbara read, "This confirms my request for a change of house-keepers. As I told you on the phone this morning, circumstances have arisen that make it impossible for me to have Nora working with me. I do not want her to enter my apartment again and will appreciate any efforts you can make in that direction. I want to assure you that this is not a matter of theft or damages, and I ask you to not tell Nora I requested the change. Thank you very much. As we agreed on the phone, I will expect to see a replacement at the regular time next Friday."

"Wow! I wonder what that's all about," Ellen said. "Do you think this could have anything to do with Laura's absence?"

Karen shook her head slowly, trying to make sense of what she had heard. "I can't imagine. I've lived across the hall from her for two years and have never heard anything unpleasant going on between them. I think Nora's great. She comes to my apartment on Friday afternoons after she's finished at Laura's. She's always cheerful and does a fine job. She even cleans the yucky disposal cover every week."

"Have any of you seen Nora this week?" Barbara asked.

"No, but she's not on this floor until Friday. She cleans at the cottages earlier in the week. I don't usually see her unless I happen to run into her in the café when she's eating lunch with her friends. I haven't heard anything about any change, and I assume she'll be at my apartment as usual on Friday."

Harriet was frowning. "I don't see that this has anything to do with Laura's absence. And I don't think it's any of our business. Maybe we should just drop it."

The room was quiet. No one agreed with her. They noted that everything in the living room seemed in order. It was a tasteful mix of contemporary furnishings and a few antiques Laura had probably inherited. A bromeliad with multicolored leaves thrived in a floor vase under a window. Books neatly lined some shelves, and even the magazines on the coffee table were carefully fanned out.

"It doesn't look like she left in a great hurry," Barbara said. "Everything's very orderly here, and it's the same in the other rooms. Come along. We'll show you what we found there."

They filed into the guest bedroom, which doubled as an office. Sandra noticed the computer on the cherry desk beside a matching office swivel chair. "The computer's off. That could indicate

Laura planned to go away. I don't turn my computer off unless I'm not going to be using it for a while and certainly when I'm going away."

"It seems to me you should always turn your computer off if you're not using it. It's a waste of electricity," Karen said. She was happy she didn't have to worry about a computer; she had never been bitten by that bug and had no intention of getting bitten despite her children's urging. Her trusty Smith-Corona typewriter had always been sufficient for writing her columns and communicating with colleagues at her various volunteer organizations. She was convinced that computers altered the way humans interacted and that thank-you notes, for example, should always be handwritten. One reason she volunteered so much was that she preferred working with people rather than machines.

Sandra, well aware of Karen's aversion to computers, smiled. "It's okay to leave it on. A computer doesn't use much electricity at all, especially if it's just sitting there."

Barbara smiled and started toward the other bedroom. "Karen and I need to show you something else, and then all of us have to decide what to do."

They followed her down the short hall to Laura's bedroom. End tables flanked a queen-sized bed neatly made up with pillows and a quilted coverlet in muted colors matching the window drapes. The chest of drawers and a small, comfortable recliner completed the picture of a tasteful retreat.

Barbara directed everyone's attention to the red message light flashing rapidly on the phone. The blinking number indicated that three messages had been recorded. "Do you think we should listen to the messages, or is that too intrusive?" she asked. "As a lawyer, I'm concerned about her privacy rights, but as her friend, I'm much more concerned about her welfare. Two of the messages are mine. That third one might be helpful."

Sandra broke the brief silence. "I say let's listen. It could give us a clue as to where she's gone."

Everyone agreed.

Barbara pushed the button. "You have one old message and two new messages."

They heard Barbara's cheerful voice say, "Hey, Laura, it's Tuesday night and we're at the table. Wake up if you're asleep and come on down." Barbara's voice came on again. "I guess you're not there. We're going ahead with dinner. Please give me a call when you get this message. Thanks."

"Those were my two messages. That means Laura heard the other message but didn't erase it.

We'll have to press the button again to hear it. Are we still up for that?"

"I say yes. We can't stop now," Sandra said. Harriet nodded. The others murmured in agreement.

Barbara pushed the message button again. "You have three old messages."

They heard a deep, male voice with an Italian accent. "Bellisima Laura, Io voglio—sorry—I mean, beautiful Laura, I really need to talk with you. I know you received my letter. I saw Roberto two days ago, and he said you had told him I had written to you. He said you weren't happy about the letter."

Barbara raised her hand to her mouth and glanced at the others.

The pitch of his voice increased. He sounded frantic. "I'm sorry to make you not happy, but I must talk to you now. I have not the time, so we have to get together. I am hoping it will be today. Please call me at this number." He gave an international cell phone number as the words lapsed into what must have been Italian, and then there was only background noise before the phone cut off. Barbara turned off the message replay button.

The women stared at each other in silence.

Ellen sat on the bed and jumped up quickly, realizing it was Laura's bed. She stared at the phone. "I can't believe what I just heard. What in the world's going on? That was scary. Did any of you recognize his voice?"

A couple of them said no quietly while others just looked at each other. They began to feel uncomfortable and a little embarrassed to find themselves in Laura's bedroom and involved in her personal life.

Karen suggested they go across the hall to her apartment. "We can mull over this a bit. I'll lock Laura's door on our way out."

"Good idea. We need to talk, but not here," Barbara said. "I'll run to my apartment for a bottle of wine. I think we could use it."

"No need," Karen replied. "I have white if that's okay, and iced tea."

Karen's apartment was softly lit—pleasant but unpretentious. It was comfortably furnished with what she had brought with her. The four settled onto the sofa and armchairs while Karen placed glasses on a side table. The drinks were cool, soothing. The women began to relax. Ellen quietly recalled what they had seen and heard.

"I know the phone call was very troubling, but it may be nothing to get concerned about," Harriet said. "I think we should back off and let events take their course. We don't want to end up looking foolish or find ourselves in trouble for intruding in Laura's affairs."

Barbara took a large swallow of her wine—one did not casually disagree with Harriet. "I don't agree with you, Harriet. I have a real feeling something's wrong. It doesn't make sense she'd just disappear."

"Let's not argue about our feelings," Karen said. "Let's look at the facts, the evidence, and then decide what we can do about it."

"I don't see that we should do anything," Harriet said.

Karen was undismayed. She mentioned Laura's uncharacteristic and unexpected absence from dinner and their failure to find an explanation at Oak Hall or in her apartment. "Then there was the note about Nora and the really strange phone message. Speaking for myself, I have lots of questions but no answers and no ideas what to do now."

Everyone was silent. Their worried frowns reflected their frustration and anxiety.

Ellen broke the silence. "When I was teaching and had a particularly difficult problem student,

I tried to find someone such as a student counselor who could help me find out what was wrong. Maybe we can't solve this by ourselves. Maybe we need someone to help us. We can't even agree there's a problem!"

Karen looked at Ellen with relief. "You're right, Ellen. Great idea. But whom can we ask?"

"It should be someone who knows us and Laura," Barbara said.

"Someone we can trust," added Ellen.

"And who knows Oakwood Village," Sandra said.

"Someone discreet," Harriet said.

"Who has dealt with unusual problems," Karen said.

"How about Stephanie?" Ellen asked. They all knew Dr. Stephanie Morrison, an Oakwood resident who was a tall, handsome woman actively involved on the board of trustees of the regional hospital.

"Stephanie is all those things we've mentioned," Barbara said, "but I think she's much too pleased with herself to spend her valuable time on this. Besides, I think she's away in the Berkshires with her family. How about the Oakwood chaplain?"

That idea met with immediate disagreement.

"Oh no. This isn't his area of expertise," Harriet said. "He's here to conduct religious programs and help those who are ill or need help with life problems, not to look for missing people."

Sandra, who had been silently listening, said, "Let's ask Robert Symonds. He knows Laura and all of us, and he seems very discreet."

Barbara jumped up from the couch nearly spilling her drink. "Yes!"

The others nodded in agreement. Robert would be perfect. Barbara suggested they invite him over right then.

"Let's give her tonight to turn up," Harriet said. "She might have gone to the movies or gone out to dinner with someone. Let's not get anyone else involved yet."

They all agreed to have Sandra call him the next morning if Laura had not returned.

Somewhat reassured, they finished their drinks and went home to bed.

CHAPTER THREE

Enter Robert

Getting older is a matter of adjusting one's expectations. When I was young, I aimed to win tennis tournaments. Now I aim to flex one knee a quarter of an inch.

—BILLIE JEAN KING

Robert Symonds's phone rang at 8:30 that morning. He had sat up late the night before watching a previously recorded *Masterpiece Mystery* episode. It was one of the few series he enjoyed. Though he found most television a waste of time and dreaded becoming a couch potato, he enjoyed that particular series. Every now and then, an episode reminded him of the exciting life he had left behind when he retired to Oakwood.

He was coming to terms with his new life. He recalled that his mother, once a distinguished Shakesperean actress, had talked of this time of life as the sunset years. He was beginning to understand what she meant. He wished he could accept them as philosophically as she had. He had his health and his wits and the security provided by Oakwood, but he felt an urge to embark on a new enterprise. He recalled that the poet had written in *Ulysses*, "Some work of noble note, may yet be done." *But what?* he asked himself.

The phone rang. "Hello?"

"It's Sandra. Hope I didn't wake you." She knew that some of Oakwood's denizens were apt to sleep late. "I'm calling with a rather unusual request. Would you be willing to meet with the Tuesday Table Ladies this morning? We need your advice about a puzzling and perhaps urgent problem. We think you can help us."

"Of course I will if you think I can be of help," he replied, always a gentleman.

Sandra sounded relieved. "Please join us at nine thirty in the small-events room where we can talk in private. Is that too soon for you?"

"I can be there at nine thirty." He thought it sounded rather pressing.

Robert Symonds was a charming man, so they said, and yet the few who knew him well also knew his greatest asset was a razor-sharp intellect. A shrewd judge of people, he had been an invaluable member of the State Department. At Oakwood, his comfortable cottage was tastefully furnished with his books and possessions he had picked up during his world travels. He had never married though women still found him attractive. The truth was that since his early days at the U.S. embassy in Rome, he had not met another person with whom he wanted to share his life.

In his retirement, he enjoyed his own company and the occasional invitations to join other residents at dinner. Laura had invited him to an occasional Tuesday meal with her five friends. He liked the relative anonymity of his life there, but he missed the challenge and intrigue of his former life, which was in marked contrast to the order and peace of Oakwood.

Oakwood was situated on what was left of an old forest. Its driveway was lined with impressive oak trees that had given the estate its name. It was on the old River Road, which linked a number of fishing villages. The large, redbrick building with tall, white columns and white shutters sat comfortably among the trees like an English mansion in a Jane Austen novel. It had retained its original name, Oak Hall, and had a large lobby area with a piano and a number of seating groups as well as a library, chapel, administrative offices, auditorium, and another dining room. Oak Hall, originally a wealthy Maryland planter's mansion, had been expanded and converted to a retirement community some twenty years earlier.

To its right were the recently built health care units, and to the left were three large apartment buildings—Albemarle, Baltimore, and Calvert. All were linked to Oak Hall with covered walkways so residents could move easily from building to building in bad weather.

Along the riverbank on either side of the Riverview dining room were a number of two-bedroom cottages for those who, like Robert, wanted a view of the river, more room, and greater privacy. Between Oak Hall and the health care center was the recreation center with an art studio, a large swimming pool and hot tub, a wide selection of the latest exercise equipment, and a pool table. All the buildings were redbrick with white trim to complement Oak Hall's original architecture.

Robert quickly made his bed and cleared the remains of his breakfast. It was still chilly at that hour, so he put on the old duffle coat he had bought in London. He locked his door and set off on the short walk to the main building.

The women were seated around a table, which held six cups and a large container of coffee, a pot of tea, and a pitcher of cream. Barbara stood to greet him. "Oh Robert, thanks for coming. We're so glad you agreed to help. We're at our wits' end as to what to do, and since you've known Laura for a long time, we thought—"

"Laura?" Robert was surprised. "You mean Laura Lambert? Has anything happened to her?"

Barbara hesitated. "Robert, Laura is missing, and we don't know what to do."

Karen jumped in. "We've tried to find her, and we found some things we can't explain. We're worried about her. Sandy, fill him in."

Sandy related to Robert in detail all the events since dinner the night before. Robert listened and asked a few questions the women could not answer. At first, he had felt there might be a simple explanation. He knew that in their small, close-knit community, it would be easy to blow things out of proportion. He noticed that Harriet seemed to be of the same opinion based on her demeanor, but the others appeared to be genuinely worried about their missing friend.

He liked the Tuesday Table Ladies. They were successful, intelligent women who were not likely to have asked him to meet with them without good cause. He had met Laura during his time in Rome many years earlier and had been pleasantly surprised to find her at Oakwood these many years later. They never talked about that time and what had happened there. They were different people now.

But Robert was taken aback when Sandra said the man who had left the message had had an Italian accent. He felt sure it was probably Eduardo, whom he had bumped into just three days earlier and who had mentioned he was looking for Laura. *Why is he here? Could this have something to do with her disappearance? The Eduardo I knew in Rome was young and impulsive. What's he like now?*

Robert told the women he would take a fresh look at the situation and work with them to find answers to at least some of their questions. That would help them decide if there was a serious problem or if they were simply blowing up a molehill to create a mountain.

The newly formed band of amateur detectives discussed their next steps.

"Fortunately, I have an almost free day today," Robert said. "I'll follow up on some of the things you've told me just in case you missed something. Would that help?"

They were relieved. Since Karen had the key to Laura's apartment and Barbara knew more than the others did about Laura's past, they were designated the principal liaisons with Robert.

"We'll keep you informed," Karen assured the other women. "And it's important that we all share anything we find out."

Everyone agreed to meet the next morning. Sandra said she would make arrangements to use the same room. "We'll meet again at nine thirty unless Laura turns up in the meantime."

They turned off the lights of the windowless conference room and left.

CHAPTER FOUR

Nora's Story

*Someone can be as beautiful on the outside as
on the inside, but when he or she betrays
your trust, that person becomes the ugliest person
in the world.*

—ANONYMOUS

Robert wanted to start immediately. He and Karen went to Laura's apartment. He had not been in her apartment before and could not have imagined he would have entered it without her invitation. Though they had met briefly many years before, they had been casual acquaintances. When he moved to Oakwood, he had been surprised to find her living there. They had dinner together occasionally, sometimes with the Tuesday Table Ladies or other groups, but their conversations had been limited to small talk and current happenings; he didn't feel he really knew her.

But his primary concerns were the phone message and the note about the housekeeper. First the message. Karen led him down the short hall to Laura's bedroom. She went to check out the closet as he pushed the message button. Unfortunately, Laura's caller ID had not been activated; that would have been helpful, he thought. He strained to hear the caller's voice over the background noise. Sounds indicated that he had been in a public place; people were talking in the background, and the echoes indicated a large room, but he couldn't tell if it was a hotel lobby, an airport or a train station, or somewhere else.

He listened to the message again to affirm his first impression. Yes, it was a man perhaps a little younger than he was. The accent was Italian, as the women had said. He recognized the particular inflections and phrasing evident in the voice on the recording. It did sound like the Eduardo he had so recently spoken to, but he was startled by the frantic tone. After a third replay, Robert concluded it was almost certainly Eduardo, but he decided not to share that information just yet; he wanted to think about it.

Robert noticed a *New York Times* crossword puzzle and pen on an end table next to a comfortably worn leather chair. Even if he had not known Laura, he could have told from the small indentations in the seat that she was a slim woman.

As they walked to the kitchen, he told Karen, "It always amazes me that there are people in this world who do puzzles with pens. I think it's either a sign of pretense, intellect, or self-confidence." Her puzzle was unfinished. He wasn't sure which applied to Laura.

Karen smiled. "I always use a crossword dictionary."

He read the strange note about the housekeeper. "Does Nora usually clean for Laura?"

"Yes she does. She helps me too. I never knew about any problems between the two of them. This is a real surprise. Do you know Nora? "

"I know who she is, and she'd recognize me. She's the housekeeper for my next-door neighbors, the Buchanans. Perhaps I can talk with Nora and see what this is all about. At this point, it's hard for me to see any connection between this note and Laura's absence, but there may be one."

Robert gazed around the living room thoughtfully. His sister had always teased him about being a closet decorator, but he had ignored her. He enjoyed looking at other people's homes and apartments to see what styles they had chosen and how their décor reflected their interests and tastes. It had helped him to assess the character of some of the diplomats he had dealt with in his working days. *Anything here that can tell me more about this woman who has disappeared leaving her friends in a state of anxiety?* He did not know very much about the young Laura he had met over fifty years ago and had not learned much more since becoming reacquainted with her at Oakwood.

The wall closest to the door was lined with bookshelves holding a variety of reading material— from Chaucer to Tom Clancy. On another wall were family photos, and on the far wall in a little niche was an old relic of sorts that looked out of place among the colorful paintings and modern wall hangings. Robert moved closer to get a good look at what seemed a very old religious icon, perhaps from the twelfth or thirteenth century; it was similar to some he had seen in the Vatican Museum. He thought about turning it around to see if something was inscribed on the back but stopped when he saw some cracks in the ornate frame.

He scanned the room. "Did you ladies find anything amiss when you came into the apartment? I don't see anything out of order here."

"Oh no. And we didn't move anything. I've just been looking in her bedroom closet and didn't notice anything unusual. There are a couple of suitcases there, but there's space enough for other bags, so she could have taken one or more. I don't know whether any clothes are gone, but everything's neat, nothing disorderly."

"We don't seem to be finding any answers here. I think we should move along."

Karen and Robert went their separate ways after securing the apartment. To take her mind off her anxiety and inspired by the neat appearance of Laura's closet, Karen decided to organize her own closet by creating summer clothes and winter clothes sections. Her military father had instilled in her the idea that there was a place for everything and everything should be in its place.

Robert wanted to confirm that Laura had not signed out and to find out if anyone had seen her leave. He headed to the front desk in Oak Hall, Oakwood's nerve center, so to speak, where staff members had answers to almost any question. Residents and visitors alike went to the front desk to give or receive information, request transportation, or ask for help if they happened to lock themselves out of their residences. It was also the place where residents signed out if they would be away overnight or longer.

Robert casually approached the woman at the desk. "Good morning, Brenda. Would you please check the sign-out book to see about my friend Laura Lambert? I'm wondering when she's returning."

Brenda obliged with a pleasant smile. "Good morning, Mr. Symonds." She opened her book. "Okay, here's her sheet. She left yesterday. It says she's visiting friends and gives her cell phone as a contact number. But there's no return date."

Robert was surprised to hear that there was a sheet in the book; he was sure that the Tuesday Table Ladies had said that there hadn't been one there. In addition, he was disappointed because there was no new information; he knew the women had decided that Laura's cell phone had been turned off. Barbara had tried numerous times to contact Laura, but Laura's mailbox had always been full.

Brenda sensed his disappointment. "John might know more than I do, but he's on break. Maybe you should come back later when he's here."

Robert thanked her and walked away, his calm demeanor masking his confusion. Having reached a roadblock at the desk, he decided to find Nora. He was able to track her down in short order with the help of the Buchanans, his neighbors who gave him her cell phone number.

Robert asked Nora if she would be willing to meet with him and talk about a mutual acquaintance, being careful to not mention any names. He suggested they meet in the small card room close to the café at 12:45. Nora agreed. He knew the room would be empty in the early afternoon.

Nora was nervous when she walked in and saw him at a table. He rose and greeted her cordially. "Hello! I'm glad to see you."

"Good morning, Mr. Symonds. I guess it should be good afternoon by now. The morning went by so quickly."

"Indeed it did. I thank you for taking time to meet with me at such short notice."

They sat across from each other. Nora was on the edge of her chair, clasping and unclasping her hands. Sensing her anxiety, Robert wanted to put her more at ease. "Isn't it about time for Buster's walk?"

"So you know Buster too!" Nora smiled. "I guess everyone in the cottages knows Buster." The Buchanans' friendly, feisty terrier was popular in the neighborhood.

Their shared laugh reduced the tension. Robert leaned forward and spoke in a calm tone. He told Nora that some of Laura Lambert's friends had become concerned about Laura in the last couple of days. "They know you've been Laura's housekeeper for months and thought you might be of help."

Nora had gasped when Robert mentioned Laura's name. She sat up. "Mr. Symonds, I did work for her, but I've been transferred to someone else. I don't know why. But I do have concerns about Mrs. Lambert."

"Yes, I know they do shift people around from time to time. But her friends have been anxious to get hold of her, so any information you have could be helpful."

Nora was soothed by his calm, comforting tone. She sat back. "I don't know where she might be right now, but Mrs. Lambert and I go back a long way. I've never told anyone about this before, but I'll tell you what I know about her.

"It started years ago. I didn't used to live around here. I'm from Pennsylvania, way off at the other end. My dad died when I was little, and I was an only child. Mom wasn't even thirty then, and she didn't know how to do anything to make a living for us.

"My dad had been her high school sweetheart. He worked in the mills in Donora, along the Monongahela River near Pittsburgh. They never thought about anyone going to college 'cause there was always work in the mills for the men. And the girls almost always were mothers within a year of getting married and took to baking cookies and knitting. That was what they all did around there.

"My parents were so fond of that whole area that they named me Donora for the town where their ancestors had grown up. I was teased about my name by my grade school classmates and asked my parents many times why they'd given me such a stupid name. Ever since I got out of school, I've called myself Nora, and I legally changed it to Nora."

She barely took a breath before continuing.

"When my dad died, Mom and I had to go live with my aunt Nan in Philadelphia. My mom had never gotten along well with her sister, but we couldn't keep up our house payments and needed a place to live. Aunt Nan was married to Uncle Bud, a lawyer and a politician of sorts. They seemed to be well off, certainly by our standards, but they were cheap in strange ways, like taking sugar packets from restaurants instead of buying their own. They did the same thing with artificial sweeteners and ketchup packets.

"They lived extravagantly on the outside, always trying to impress their friends at the club and acting as if they were better than us. At first, my mom and I did most of the work around the house, and it was pretty hard and lonely for a time, but Uncle Bud started treating me more like a niece. He made me feel like I belonged to the family. He even told me I was in his will. I loved the attention!" Nora blushed. Her voice softened. "I loved the attention."

Robert waited a moment for Nora to compose herself, but he wondered what all that had to do with Laura. "What happened to bring you to Oakwood?"

"I know this is a long story, Mr. Symonds, but I'm coming to that. After I graduated from high school, I took a secretarial course. I went to work in Uncle Bud's office. I was in a back office doing a lot of filing and mimeographing. I liked the work and the gals in the office. He had all sorts of clients.

"Things went along fine until one day when a woman came into the office crying about her abusive marriage. She wanted a divorce. Well, it didn't take long for that woman to end Uncle Bud's marriage. In eighteen months, she had her divorce and my Uncle Bud. He divorced Aunt Nan, and there went my inheritance and our security. In the end, Aunt Nan made us leave.

"Mom moved back to Donora, but I couldn't stand it there. My best friend at the office had a sister who worked here in Maryland. Through her, I learned that Mrs. Lambert had moved to Oakwood, so I got a job here."

Robert was becoming impatient. Nora hadn't answered his question. He came to the point. "Your story's a sad one, Nora. I'm sorry for your problems. I wanted to speak to you because I thought you might know something about where Mrs. Lambert is. Her friends prevailed upon me to talk to you, and that's why I'm here today."

Nora looked directly at him. "You might find this hard to believe, but the woman who stole my Uncle Bud was your friend Laura Lambert."

CHAPTER FIVE

A Confidential Tale

Love looks not with the eyes, but with the mind;
And therefore is winged Cupid painted blind.
                    —WILLIAM SHAKESPEARE

R obert pondered what Nora had told him as
he walked through the lobby. On the surface, Nora's story seemed to have little connection
to Laura's disappearance, but he couldn't be sure.
Nora had claimed that as far as she knew, Laura had
not recognized her from her uncle's office and Nora
hadn't told anyone at Oakwood about her feelings
about Laura. *Could there be some other reason for
Laura's replacing Nora?* Robert thought Laura could
have sensed Nora's attitude toward her and had been
disturbed enough to dismiss her. *Would Nora be*

capable of physical violence toward Laura? She had told him she hoped that by coming to Oakwood, she might eventually be able to expose the truth about Laura, but perhaps her real intentions were more menacing. Nora had still been agitated but had seemed relieved when he stood up, thanked her for sharing her feelings, and assured her it would not affect her job in any way.

Robert saw John, the regular day attendant, was back on duty. "I understand Mrs. Lambert signed out yesterday. Did she happen to mention where she was going?" he asked.

"No," John replied. "In fact, I didn't even see her. I went into the grill to get a cup of coffee about ten this morning, and when I came back, the sign-out sheet was on the desk, so I filed it in the folder. I never saw her at all."

"Did you say *this* morning? Wasn't the sheet dated yesterday?"

"Yes. I thought that was strange, but I figured maybe she'd just put down the wrong date." John pulled the paper out of the notebook and handed it to Robert.

"Was there anyone else in the lobby then?'

"Not that I noticed. That's why I thought it was a good time to get my coffee. Everything was quiet."

Robert looked at the sheet and copied down Laura's cell number. "Is it unusual for residents to check out without giving a return date?"

"It happens sometimes when they aren't really sure when they'll get back or don't want Security checking their apartments if they haven't returned by the date they said they would."

"Do you have any old sign-out sheets that she might have signed in the past?"

"No. After they check back in, we toss the old ones. Otherwise, we'd soon run out of space to file them."

"Makes sense," Robert said. "I'm used to government records that they seem to keep forever in a cave somewhere. Now, they're all stored in the cloud."

"One other thing," John said. "Mrs. Lambert got an outside call yesterday morning. A woman called and asked if Laura Lambert was here. She had an address but no phone number, so I put her through to Mrs. Lambert. She sounded really excited, which is why I remember it. Hope that helps."

"Thanks again, John. You've been very helpful. By the way, is Mrs. Evans in her office?"

"Yes, I believe so. She just returned from a meeting a few minutes ago."

Robert walked down the hallway to the open door of the executive director's office. "Do you have a minute, Cathy? I need some advice."

"Well that's a switch. Sure, come on in, Rob."

Catherine Evans had been the executive director of Oakwood for about ten years. She was very popular among the residents because of her warmth and helpfulness. Her open-door policy was a far cry from that of the previous administrator, who had been much more formal in dealing with the residents. Formerly the nursing administrator at a large hospital in DC, she had changed direction after her husband's sudden death when she was only fifty-five. She had chosen the equally challenging but quieter and less-hectic environment at Oakwood. She was ideally suited for the position. Her leadership skills resulted in a smooth-running organization.

A few residents were aware that Robert and Catherine had known each other before he moved to Oakwood, but no one was aware of how close their relationship had been. Cathy's husband, Gary, had been Robert's college roommate, and Robert had served as the best man at their wedding. When Gary unexpectedly suffered a fatal heart attack, Robert was one of the first friends she called. She and Gary had no children, and her parents were deceased, so

Robert served as the older brother she'd never had. His friendship with Cathy was one of the reasons he had come to Oakwood.

They chose to keep the true nature of their friendship private from the residents for several reasons. Of course they wanted to avoid any charges of favoritism, but more important, they recognized that most of the residents were inveterate romantics and terrible gossips who would immediately read a romantic relationship into their friendship.

Actually, what they had was much more valuable than a romance. They were comfortable old friends who could be completely frank and honest with each other without any pretense. Cathy used Robert as a sounding board to try out ideas she had about improvements to Oakwood or to discuss problems with the staff. Robert liked to reminisce about the old days and tell her amusing stories about the pranks he and Gary had carried out at Harvard.

Since they preferred to talk in private and did not want to be seen going into each other's cottages though they lived only three doors apart, they got together from time to time at carefully selected restaurants in nearby communities where they were not likely to run into Oakwood residents.

The two agreed to meet for dinner at one of their favorite Italian restaurants where they could talk freely without being interrupted by her secretary or other staff members.

❦

Over dinner that evening, Robert outlined the mystery of Laura's disappearance, her friends' concerns, and his talk with Nora. "I don't suppose there's anything you can do officially?" he asked.

"Absolutely not. Since there's a sign-out sheet, even if there's a question about it, I really can't intrude on her privacy. That's especially because Mrs. Lambert seems to be a very private person and a lawyer to boot. From what you say, many of her friends don't know a lot about her. Our residents are independent adults, free to come and go as they please. Only when there's a question of dementia would we have a right to pry into a resident's whereabouts if he or she has signed out."

"That's what I thought," said Robert, "but it seemed important to let you know what's going on especially since they've involved me in this. Incidentally, do you know anything else about Nora?"

"Only that she came with outstanding references, though she seemed overqualified for a housekeeping job. I have no idea why Laura wanted to change housekeepers. I read what she said on the work order. The staff brought it to me because it was such an unusual request, but I saw no reason to refuse it, so another housekeeper has already been assigned to her apartment. I certainly knew nothing of Nora's connection to her."

Cathy took one of the macaroons the waiter had brought with their coffee. "What about the man's voice on the answering machine? Do you have any idea what that was about?"

"Yes, I'm pretty sure I know who it is, especially since he mentioned talking to 'Roberto' last week. That's another story. Perhaps I should fill you in on that too. As far as I know, he may be one of the few people alive who know what happened in Rome."

"It sounds serious." Cathy's curiosity was aroused.

"It certainly was at the time. It was my second posting with the State Department, and I'd been in Rome about a year. One morning, the ambassador called me into his office and told me, 'Take care of this mess,' as he put it. He'd received a distress call from an old friend of his, a prominent physician in Boston. It seemed his eighteen-year-old daughter had just called her parents with the news she'd gotten married three weeks earlier to a young Italian race car driver. She was in Rome for the summer with a couple of friends to take an intensive Italian language course. She had apparently met Eduardo at a party, and they immediately knew they were meant for each other."

"That sounds like an eighteen-year-old. How old was he?"

"About twenty-one or twenty-two. They were both pretty immature."

"Why on earth did her parents let her go to Rome on her own?"

"I had the impression they were both busy that summer. Her mother, a professor at Boston University, was finishing up a book on eighteenth-century English literature and fighting a deadline. Her dad was chairing a search committee that was looking for a new dean for the medical school. Laura told me they were glad to have the summer free to work. It was convenient for them to send her off to Rome. Laura was an only child and pretty used to getting her own way. They probably thought she'd have an interesting summer, learn some Italian, and see the sights. No one anticipated what actually happened."

"So what did you do?"

"The ambassador said Laura and Eduardo were coming to the embassy that afternoon, and he had to attend an important conference, so it was up to me. Apparently, her father had exploded when he heard the news and threatened to take the next flight to Rome. Laura begged him not to come, and he agreed provided she went to the embassy that afternoon. Then he got on the phone to the ambassador and asked him, 'Please take care of this.'

"I have to admit I was stunned when the newlyweds came into my office. She was one of the most beautiful eighteen-year-olds I'd ever seen. Long, blond hair, perfect skin, and huge, azure-blue eyes. She could have modeled for any agency in the country. Though she was so young, I might have been attracted to her myself if I hadn't already been involved with someone else.

"And he was just as striking—tall, dark, and with that slight swagger you see in men who are aware of their impact on others. I could see why they were so attracted to each other. The question was whether the attraction went beyond the surface."

"How did you handle them?"

"I was very gentle with them and let them tell their story. They had met at a party of a friend of his, talked to each other all evening, and left together. She had told her friends she'd meet up with them later at their apartment, which she did at four in the morning. Her friends tried to convince her to slow down the romance, that they were moving too fast, but she was adamant. She couldn't let this opportunity for love pass her by. Eventually, she stopped going to class and spent all her time with Eddie, following him from race track to race track.

"The young man, Eddie G as he was called by the press, was all the rage in Rome that summer and for years after that. He'd won a number of prestigious races, was tall and handsome, and all the girls were chasing him. He was a natural for the press. The newspapers loved him and played up every win to the hilt. It was easy to see how Laura had fallen for this handsome and charming young man. In fact, I liked him myself. I knew it wouldn't be easy to persuade her to go home."

Cathy was listening intently.

"Fortunately, they'd told no one they were married. Even her friends didn't know. She went back to their apartment every night, though sometimes it was more like early morning. She wanted to tell her parents first and was afraid they'd hear about it from a reporter if the press got hold of the story. She finally got the nerve to call them. Her father's reaction was exactly what she'd feared."

"How in the world did you get through to them?"

"I had one advantage. He spoke almost no English, and her Italian was rudimentary. Obviously, their mutual attraction wasn't based on their intellectual conversations. I spoke to each one separately without interruptions."

Robert sighed. "I spoke to her first in English, explaining what her life would be like as an Italian housewife. While Eddie was traveling around Europe on the race circuit, she'd be stuck in an apartment with one, then two, then more kids cooking and cleaning. I pointed out that all Italian husbands expected large families and that the wives stayed home to run things. I drew on every negative stereotype about Italian men I could come up with and managed to paint a pretty grim picture of her future in Italy, not one that would appeal to a beautiful and spoiled American teenager. It had the intended effect. I felt guilty but figured it was best for her in the long run. Besides, it was my assignment. I didn't know what else to do."

"But what about him? Why did he give up?"

"While she was contemplating the dreary picture of her future in Rome I'd drawn for her, I spoke to him in Italian pointing out that once the press found out about his marriage, there would be a week or so of intense publicity and then they'd drop him and look for another hot, young driver who was single. I told him the press considered married men as generally boring. He'd no longer be the handsome, sexy bachelor they had been interested in, and there were plenty of those on the race circuit waiting to take his place. I told him even the girls would lose interest in someone who was no longer available.

"It was obviously an aspect of the situation he hadn't considered. I left them alone for a few minutes to talk it over and say their good-byes. I drove her to her apartment to pack her things and got her on a nonstop to Boston that night. I assumed her father arranged for an annulment, and we never spoke of it again. Then Laura married a few years later. Looking back, I think they both had had second thoughts about their impetuous marriage."

He paused thoughtfully for a while. "I used to run into her from time to time when she and her husband were living in DC. We'd meet at parties and embassy events. She never seemed comfortable with me, but she was always polite and charming.

I was never sure whether she resented my interference in her brief first marriage or whether she was actually somewhat relieved I'd gotten her out of it. Perhaps a little of both. She and her new husband seemed very happy together.

"Unfortunately, like your Gary, he died too soon. I know she married again, but that ended in divorce. I assume that was the divorce Nora was upset about. But Nora's story about Laura's stealing her uncle from his wife just doesn't ring true. I don't think that's the kind of situation Laura would stumble into at that stage of her life. I'd think she'd learned her lesson in Rome and wouldn't make more complications for herself."

"It was shortly after her divorce that she came to Oakwood," Cathy said. "There was certainly no lovesick lawyer following her here. But why did she go to Philadelphia for her divorce? Why didn't she use her own law firm?"

"Perhaps she didn't want her friends to know the messy details. Apparently, it was an abusive situation. You know how private she is. I'm not sure she ever told anyone besides me and her parents about her marriage to Eddie."

"Speaking of him, is he the one you heard on the answering machine?"

"I'm almost sure it was. Especially since he mentioned my name. He seemed very eager to talk to her, but she had told me that she was disturbed by his letter and didn't want to discuss it. As I said before, Laura values her privacy."

"All the more reason Oakwood can't get officially involved in this unless there's real evidence that something might have happened to her," Cathy said.

They considered the situation as they sipped their coffee.

"Will you tell the Tuesday dinner group about her marriage to Eddie in the morning?" asked Cathy.

"No. I told you because I think it's important you have the whole story just in case there really is something wrong and Oakwood is affected in some way. I won't violate her privacy any more than I have to. I can tell them what Nora told me about her previous connection with Laura and her feeling that Laura had caused her to lose her possible inheritance. I can also talk to them about the sign-out sheet and its mysterious appearance on the front desk the day after she left."

"You know, something else occurs to me. You might want to ask one of the women to talk to her hairdresser. Women tell their hairdressers all kinds of things, including their hopes and plans. Most hairdressers are pretty astute in sizing up their clients."

"Thanks. I think that might be worth pursuing."

They strolled to the parking lot. Robert agreed to keep Cathy informed of any new developments. They drove separately back to Oakwood.

CHAPTER SIX

Next Steps

When you begin to worry find something to do. Get busy being a blessing to someone; do something fruitful.

—JOYCE MEYER

R obert was up early on Thursday morning. He stood before his bathroom mirror shaving and thinking about what he could tell the Tuesday Table Ladies. He did not have much solid information. There was Nora's story, but even that needed to be verified. *Is Nora actually implicated in Laura's absence? Where is Laura? What were the circumstances of her disappearance?* Though questions remained, he realized that maybe there was a simple explanation and that this was all much ado about nothing. The sign-out sheet suggested as much. And he had done what he had said he would do in checking out the things that were worrying the women. Perhaps this was it for him. He would not refer to Eduardo's phone message; he still wanted to reflect on that. *But what's there to reflect on? It was an agitated voice from the past trying to contact a woman who didn't want to respond. Is it as simple as that? Perhaps not.*

He carefully rinsed and patted his face dry and looked in the mirror. His hair was quite grey now, not nearly as distinguished as before. But he reckoned that it looked pretty good by Oakwood's standards.

Over breakfast, he decided he would report to the women and leave it to them to pursue their investigation on their own. He wondered what their response would be. Besides being genuinely concerned about Laura, they were caught up in the mystery. Doubtless they would want to keep on searching. He wondered what he could advise them. He recalled Cathy's suggestion that they might make inquiries at the Oakwood beauty salon. That would have to be done with subtlety. He wondered which of the women was the best candidate for that assignment.

He remembered that two of them had claimed to be computer geeks. Sandra, the attractive and vibrant one, had a degree in information science.

Though Ellen was quiet and shy, she had had a career as a math teacher, and he had heard that she had once challenged Sandra to a duel on the computer. Perhaps he could ask them to see if they could find out more about Laura. Their findings might yield some useful information. It might even solve the mystery.

That left Karen, Barbara, and Harriet. He knew of course next to nothing about women's beauty salons, so he concluded those three would have to figure out how to go about it themselves. He decided that was as much as he could do. He had his own interests to pursue. He hadn't even finished reading the latest issue of the *Journal of Foreign Affairs*. He chuckled to himself recalling his roué friend who had eagerly borrowed a copy thinking it had quite a different kind of content. *It's time to meet with the ladies and get back to my routine.* He was confident it would be that simple.

❦

The women were in the activity room fortified with large cups of coffee or tea when he entered at 9:30. They fell silent as he sat. Karen handed him a welcomed cup of black coffee, and they waited impatiently while he enjoyed the first sip.

He started his report by recounting his discovery of the newly added sign-out sheet. "I wonder where it came from," Karen said.

"Did you say it wasn't signed?" Barbara asked. "You know, it might not have been put there by Laura at all."

After a pause, Harriet said, "We won't solve the mystery just sitting here. Let's hear what else Robert has to say."

Robert briefed them on his conversation with Cathy Evans. She had confirmed what he had suspected, that Oakwood had no grounds to be involved. Laura was an independent adult of sound mind with a right to come and go as she pleased. Furthermore, there was the sign-out sheet. He also told them without commenting further that he had listened to the messages. He quickly went on to Laura's note requesting Nora's reassignment.

They listened eagerly as he briefly recounted Nora's tale of Laura's apparent involvement with her uncle and the consequences for Nora's expectations of a better life. "She's very bitter about the legacy she and her mother had expected and blames Laura for it. She sees Laura as a scheming seducer of sorts."

The women's reaction was one of quiet disbelief. "That just doesn't sound like Laura," Barbara said.

"Can this have anything to do with Laura's disappearance?" asked Sandra.

"She did come to work at Oakwood, where she knew Laura was living. It was deliberate," Ellen said.

"I've been thinking," said Barbara, who had discovered the memo in Laura's kitchen asking for Nora's reassignment, "that this might explain something that has puzzled us. Suppose Laura sensed Nora's animosity and was alarmed by it. Though she couldn't have known its cause, she might have thought Nora had a bad attitude. That could explain why she didn't want Nora in her apartment."

The others nodded thoughtfully. Robert pushed back his chair decisively and said that his part was done, that it was at that point up to them.

Sandra seized the moment. "We need to decide what we should do next."

This was followed by several women complaining they were at a loss for ideas. Harriet even ventured that they had done what they could and that they should just wait for further developments.

"Not so fast," Sandra said. "There has to be something else we could be doing."

That was Robert's moment to propose that Sandra and Ellen use their computer skills to find any information about Laura that could throw light on her absence. He also floated the idea of an attempt to gather information at the beauty salon. "Who knows? You might learn something there. Hairdressers are reputed to know more about their clients' private lives and thoughts than their spouses do."

"I wouldn't go that far," Barbara said, "though I admit that some women do talk a lot and that sometimes they say more than they should. It feels good to have an understanding listener. Hairdressers, like bartenders, have learned to be sympathetic to their customers' woes. Patti does Laura's hair. I go to the salon every week for a shampoo and blow-dry. Sally does my hair, but Patti knows me, and I can talk to her. I'll go today and see what I can learn." Barbara had been careful not to mention in Robert's presence the color touch-ups that were part of Laura's routine. Every woman is entitled to her beauty secrets.

"That sounds fine." Robert drained his coffee and stood. "I think you have enough to work on. I'm happy to have you take over now."

"We'll get busy right away," Sandra said. "Thank you very much for all this information, but just in case, don't leave us completely, Robert."

Robert smiled and nodded farewell.

The five women finished their coffee and tea. They decided Robert's suggestions were sensible; they were relieved that they could take part in finding Laura.

"That's all very well as far as it goes," said Karen, "but do you realize Robert hardly mentioned the strange telephone message? That makes me uneasy. Come to think of it, the message alluded to a Roberto. Don't you think it odd that our well-traveled friend is named Robert? Quite a coincidence I'd say!"

"I think that's going too far. We should stick to the facts," Harriet said in a scolding tone.

"We don't have many of those," Karen said, trying to quell her annoyance with Harriet.

Sensing they were on the brink of a frustrating argument, Ellen, ever the peacemaker, said, "Okay, ladies, Sandy and I will start our inquiry this afternoon. Is that okay with you, Sandy?"

Sandra replied eagerly, "Sure! Your computer or mine?"

"Let's eat together tonight and see if we've made any progress," Barbara said.

All agreed it was a good idea.

"I'll make the reservation. Is six okay?"

CHAPTER SEVEN
The Search Begins

The fantastic advances in the field of electronic communication constitute a great danger to the privacy of the individual.

—EARL WARREN

O n the way to Ellen's apartment, she and Sandra discussed what they should look for first in their computer search. Both had been using computers since the late 1970s; Sandra had been the proud owner of one of the first TRS-80s back then and recognized the possibilities for the new technology. After returning to the University of Pennsylvania for an advanced degree in computer science, she had enjoyed a productive career as an IT consultant for small businesses.

Ellen had been a math teacher when computers were introduced in her high school; she was uncomfortable knowing some students were more adept than the teachers were at using the new machines.

She too returned to college for a master's in information technology and became the computer specialist for her school district.

Ellen's apartment was neat and orderly—no doilies or frills on the contemporary and comfortable furniture. Magazines on the coffee table were not devoted to household hints but focused on scientific subjects and computers. Pictures of her children at various ages sat beside her favorite volumes on bookshelves.

The two moved quickly through the living room to the den, excited about their quest. They planned to use Ellen's computer and share information with Sandra's laptop. "First, we have to find out about this Uncle Bud," Sandra said. "He seems to be the link between Nora and Laura. We need his name. Did you ever hear Laura talk about someone named Bud?"

"I don't see her a lot except on Tuesday nights, and you know she doesn't share much about what went on in her life before she came to Oakwood."

"You're right about that," Sandra said. "But wait a minute. Barbara used to work with Laura at that law firm in Washington. She might remember something that could help us. She didn't speak up this morning, but let's call her right away."

"I don't have her number in my phone, but I have my trusty Oakwood directory right here by the computer."

Barbara was at home when they called; Sandra asked if she knew anything about Laura's relationship with Nora's uncle. She switched to speakerphone. "No. I wish I did. When we worked together, Laura was married."

"Was her last name Lambert then?" Ellen asked.

"No. She was married to Mike Stockton, a really nice fellow, a lawyer with the State Department she'd met in law school. After I left the firm, she would mention him when we got together for lunch every once in a while, but after that, I lost touch with her. My husband was transferred to Baltimore, and I got busy with the kids and our new life there. A few years later, we reconnected at an AAUW convention. I thought it was funny both of us had been active in our local chapters. Anyway, Laura told me Mike had been killed the year before in a freak car accident on the Beltway. Really sad."

Sandra sighed. "So she must have married again before she met Uncle Bud. And the second husband must have been the abusive one she was divorcing."

"Did you two keep in touch during all that?" Ellen asked.

"Oh no, not at all. I loved being a full-time mom. I even dropped out of AAUW and spent my time with the Girl Scouts and PTA and other activities. I didn't meet up with Laura again until we ran into each other here at Oakwood last year. I'd been here for two years and was surprised to see her. She had this different last name, Lambert, and never really wanted to talk about the intervening years.

"Actually, I had no problem with that. Things had been pretty tough for me after my husband died. The kids had grown up and had scattered to different parts of the country. So here at Oakwood, when Laura and I are together, we talk about what's happening now or laugh about our memories of that law firm."

"I can understand that," Sandra said. "Thanks so much for your help. If you think of anything else, please let us know. Ellen's waving good-bye and thanks you too."

She hung up. "Well, that was a blind alley, interesting, but still a blind alley. At least we learned Uncle Bud's last name wasn't Lambert."

"Yes, we know what his last name is *not*, but if we're going to do a search, we need to know what it *is*," Ellen said, her voice rising a bit. "Sooo ... who might know? Oh my Lord. Of course Nora would."

"Yes of course she'd know," Sandra said, "but we can't ask *her*. She doesn't know we know anything about what she told Robert. Where else can we get the information?"

"Didn't Robert say that Nora worked in the secretarial pool in her uncle's law firm? When she applied for the job here at Oakwood, she would have put down her previous work experience. We could get the name of the firm there."

"Good idea, Ellen. But we can't exactly sashay into the personnel office and ask to look at Nora's job application."

"But Robert and Cathy seem to have a strong friendship," Ellen said. "And he's already informed her about this situation. He could ask her to give us the firm's name without involving anyone else. I bet that could work. No one would question the executive director's digging up that information."

Sandra wondered if Robert would be willing to talk to Cathy again. "Remember he said he was going to drop out of the picture and let us carry on."

But Ellen was confident Robert could be persuaded to help again with their request. "Let's get Harriet to ask him. We need to find Laura, and Harriet can be very persuasive with that indomitable will of hers. I bet he'll agree to help a little more. We're not asking him for much."

"Yes, but we have another possible option," Sandra said. "Someone could get the information directly from Nora."

"And just how in the world do you intend to wheedle it out of her?"

Sandra said, "Oh, that wouldn't be *my* job. She doesn't know me, but she knows Karen. She's been cleaning for her every Friday, and I think they're friendly. Let's ask Karen to talk with her. I bet she can come up with a discreet way to broach the subject."

Karen indeed had developed a reputation for dealing with people; she always made eye contact with those she spoke to so they felt they had her full attention.

"Tomorrow's Friday, so she could talk with her then and can make it really casual," Ellen said. "Let's talk to Karen tonight at dinner while we're sharing with all of the gals whatever we discover this afternoon. After that, we can all decide how to proceed. In the meantime, you and I need to get to work and see what we can find out with just what we know now."

They sat in front of the computer, and Ellen clicked on a browser that would not keep a record of their searches. "I guess we could start by seeing what we can find out about Laura's marital history. Maybe that'll help us find her."

CHAPTER EIGHT
Dinner

Being defeated is often a temporary condition.
Giving up is what makes it permanent.
—MARILYN VOS SAVANT

As usual, Harriet arrived a few minutes early for dinner to take her regular seat with her back to the wall. She surveyed the dining room and noted various dinner groups, including a large table celebrating a birthday complete with balloons and grandchildren as well as a number of couples and foursomes.

Martha and Henry were a twosome Harriet wondered about; they were at a corner table deep in conversation. *What's going on with those two? Serious romance blooming or just two friends who like to eat together?* She knew they had both lost spouses in the last few years and had met at a yoga class at Oakwood, but she realized that was not unusual in a retirement community. What was unusual was the way Martha seemed to gaze at Henry, giving him her full attention whenever they were together. She reminded Harriet of a lovesick teenager soulfully gazing at a high school football player, and that seemed rather ridiculous to Harriet. *Oh well, it's really none of my business.*

She turned her attention to the dramatic sunset reflected in the river. A few boats were motoring upstream trying to make it home before darkness fell. Harriet reminisced about her early years sailing her sloop on the waters of the Chesapeake. Her advancing age had reduced her boating to an occasional cruise on a friend's powerboat, a far cry from the exciting yacht club races of her youth. She had always won her share of trophies much to her delight and the dismay of the teenage boys she competed against. It was her competitive spirit and sailing prowess that first won the attention and then the admiration of her future husband. Unlike most boys, who were intimidated by her independence and competitiveness, he had welcomed the challenge. They had spent many happy afternoons racing each other across the bay and back.

After their marriage, they bought a larger sailboat and spent many of their summer weekends exploring the coves and creeks that bordered the bay and occasionally cruising down the coast to Norfolk and beyond.

That was many years ago, but the bay still held a seductive charm for her. There were more houses and marinas along the shore than before, but the water was essentially unchanged; it moved about on its own schedule, unaffected by the humans who swarmed over and around it in a variety of watercraft.

Her reverie was interrupted when Karen took her seat at the table. "We had the greatest class today," she announced. Karen was taking a course on the War of 1812 at the small private college nearby. Senior citizens had their pick of a variety of noncredit courses taught largely by retired faculty members, and many Oakwood residents took advantage of these continuing education opportunities.

"Dr. Baron had a wonderful PowerPoint presentation on the burning of Washington and the Battle of Baltimore and Fort McHenry. I really like him. He's very down to earth and makes everything so clear. He reminds me of my father, and it doesn't hurt that he's rather handsome too. He's just written a book on the history of the bay that I want to read. You should order it for the library."

Sandra and Ellen interrupted the conversation; they were eager to report what they had uncovered.

"You'll never guess how we got Uncle Bud's last name," Sandra said. "We thought we might have to ask Nora herself or have Robert get it from Cathy, who could look up her employment references, but we found it online almost by chance."

"That's great, but why don't you wait until Barbara gets here so you don't have to repeat everything?" Harriet asked as she turned to the evening's menu.

"I saw that tonight's chef's special is seared duck breast. That's my favorite," Karen said.

"I hate it when they have three entrees I like," said Sandra. "It makes it so hard to choose. That's why I like it when we have a buffet and can take a little of everything."

Emily, their server, brought wine glasses and ice water with slices of lemon. The women passed the wine around the table as they studied their menus. The seafood choice of coconut shrimp with spicy orange sauce and the meat entrée of balsamic rosemary pork tenderloin made deciding that much more difficult.

Barbara arrived with apologies for being late. "My daughter called as I was about to leave, and I just couldn't interrupt her. She was so excited about my grandson's gymnastics tournament and wanted to fill me in on all the details. I finally told her you all were waiting and I'd call her later." For Barbara, family was always the first priority.

After Emily had taken their orders, three of the women headed for the salad bar while the others started on the bowls of crab bisque Emily had brought.

When everyone was once again gathered around the table, Sandra and Ellen began their story.

"After we asked Barbara if she knew the name of Uncle Bud's law firm and she couldn't help us, we thought about asking Nora or getting it from Cathy via Robert. But then we thought first we'd try a long shot, and it paid off," Sandra reported. "I've been working on a family history and have a subscription to *Families*, a family history database. We thought it was possible that someone in Nora's family could have worked on a family tree. So many people are doing that now since more and more information is available online. And we lucked out! Apparently, a cousin of Nora's had been working on this for several years. When we typed in Nora's name, we found a complete family tree that included her parents and her aunt and uncle."

Ellen broke in. "It included her Aunt Nan's married name as well as her maiden name along with her husband's name and his parents. So we finally had Uncle Bud's whole name, and using another search engine, we found his law firm and more information about him. His second wife is named Sylvia, and they're living in Philadelphia. It looks like they were married shortly after Nora left. Apparently, after he left the law firm, they had some heavy medical expenses resulting in serious financial problems and had to file for bankruptcy, so there wouldn't have been a legacy for Nora in any case. It looks like Uncle Bud's only relationship with Laura was as her lawyer in the divorce case; he had nothing to do with Laura after that."

The two women smiled at each other and settled back into their chairs.

"It was luck that we found him," said Sandra. "Most of the time, the names of descendants who are still living aren't shown on the *Families* database, so it was unusual to be able to access Uncle Bud's name."

"Well, that's progress," Barbara said, "but Nora's apparently not aware of this other woman and still holds a grudge against Laura even if it's unwarranted. So the question is, do we tell her what you've found out? Is it fair to keep this information from her? Now that I think about it, is it possible we're already too late? I sure hope a vengeful Nora hasn't already taken some action against Laura."

Harriet spoke up. "I think we should tell Robert what we found and let him handle it. He's the one she spoke to, and I think he could give her this information if he thinks it appropriate."

The others agreed that Harriet's suggestion made sense. They were relieved to turn the decision over to Robert.

"There's one other thing," said Sandra. "We then did a search on Laura and found out that Lambert is actually her maiden name. She was listed as Laura Lambert Stockman in several professional organizations. We assume that she went back to her maiden name after she divorced her second husband. She wouldn't have wanted to keep the name of her abusive husband, Hendrix."

"Oh of course. I should have known that," said Barbara, shaking her head. "She was already married and using Stockman when I joined the firm, but she used to sign her correspondence as Laura L. Stockman."

"So that explains the name change," Karen said, reluctantly admitting to herself that computers might actually have a use after all.

"I have some other news that might be helpful," Barbara said. "I had a talk with her hairdresser, Patti, as we agreed, and I found out something that throws a different light on Laura's disappearance."

Barbara's news had to wait while Emily served their entrees and refilled the water glasses. She was assisted by another server, Kevin, a tall, lanky, good-looking young man who carried the heavy tray bearing the meals. After they left and the women started on their entrees, Barbara was ready to share her findings.

"I went to the beauty salon to speak to Patti. She was on break, so that was good timing. I told her we were wondering where Laura was and thought she might know. She didn't have an answer, but she said Laura had been there Tuesday morning and had had her hair touched up, shampooed, and set and had had a manicure. Patti thought she seemed very excited, but Laura hadn't said anything to explain it. I didn't want to make too much of a fuss, so I let it go at that. I don't think she knows anything else. But this suggests that wherever Laura went, she did so voluntarily. And there's one other thing. She made another appointment with Patti for next week."

"I can add to that," said Harriet. "I was in the garage yesterday and noticed her car was gone. I thought she might have left it outside, as she often does, so today, I drove around all the Oakwood parking lots to check them out, but there was no sign of her car. So we might have a mystery on our hands, but it doesn't look like there's a crime at this point since she seems to have left in her car on her own. I think we should mind our own business and wait until she returns and tells us where she's been. It's even possible she's off on a romantic getaway."

"You may be right," replied Sandra, "but I still have an uneasy feeling about this. If she had time to get her hair done, she certainly had time to let us know she wouldn't be at dinner. That just isn't like her. Also, if she left Tuesday afternoon, why was the sign-out form not turned in until Wednesday? And who filled it out?"

"And what about the strange voice on the telephone? I thought he sounded desperate. Do you think she actually went to meet him?" asked Ellen. The memory of that voice on the phone had kept her awake much of the night.

"I have to confess I have the answer to one of those questions," Harriet said hesitantly. "I know you probably won't like it, but it seemed to me that if you thought she had signed out, you would let it go until she returned. You were all so excited and running off in every direction looking for Laura and making a big deal out of the fact she didn't tell us she wasn't going to be at dinner, so *I* filled out the sheet and left it on the desk when John wasn't looking. I was hoping that if all of you thought Laura had signed out, you'd drop the matter. I was obviously wrong."

The others stared at her in utter disbelief. "How could you do such a thing?" Barbara asked with a frown. "What on earth possessed you to do that when you knew we were worried about her?"

"That's exactly why I did it. I thought you were all overreacting and being too dramatic about what was basically a trivial event. It all boils down to the fact that she didn't call to tell us she wasn't going to be at dinner. That's no reason to start a massive manhunt." Harriet was speaking heatedly. "Now it looks like I was right. We checked out Nora's story, and there's no obvious connection to Laura's disappearance—if you can even call it that. She had her hair done and took her car. You may think I was wrong to turn in the sign-out sheet, but I believe we should just drop the whole thing."

"Harriet may be right," Karen said. "If Laura was excited about meeting someone, she might just have neglected to call us and to fill out the sign-out sheet. I've forgotten to sign out myself at times. In fact, she might have tried to call one of us and we weren't home."

"But then why wouldn't she have left a message?" Barbara asked. "It just doesn't feel right. The guy on the phone sounded so scared and desperate. Something was clearly wrong, and it involved Laura." Barbara, who always looked for logical explanations to matters, would not be satisfied until she found one.

"And remember that Nora still thinks Laura destroyed her life," said Sandra. "We have a number of possible scenarios to think about, but we probably aren't going to figure it out now. Besides, our dinners are getting cold."

The tablemates turned their attention to the delicious food. "This duck is cooked perfectly," Sandra said, "though the green beans are a little underdone again."

"Yes, they're usually either too raw or so overdone they're mushy. I bet the chef responds to the comment cards filled out by the residents and then goes too far in the other direction," Karen said.

But Ellen was just picking at her food. She could not set aside her fears.

A few minutes later, Emily appeared to clear the table and take orders for dessert and coffee. "Tonight, we have French silk pie, cappuccino crunch sundae, cream puff, or chocolate chip cookies," she announced cheerily.

She took orders for two pies, one sundae, one cream puff, and "Just some coffee please." She removed the dishes and left to place the dessert orders.

"I suggest we drop the whole thing until Laura gets back," Harriet said. "Is anyone else going to the musical program in the ballroom after dinner? The music committee has booked a string quartet that's supposed to be very good. It's a family group with four young adults. Two of them are studying at Peabody. It should be an interesting program."

"I'm not going. I'm just not in the mood tonight," Ellen said quietly.

Since Barbara could think of no immediate steps to take, she reluctantly agreed to attend the concert with the others.

After finishing their dessert and coffee, the women walked the short distance from the Riverview dining room to Oak Hall. They paused briefly to look back at the river, almost shrouded in darkness since the sun had set. The water moving slowly downstream reflecting the lights from the shore was a beautiful sight.

"I would love to have seen this place when it was new, with guests coming up the river by boat or arriving by carriage along the old River Road," Barbara said. "It was such a different era."

"When you think about it, perhaps it wasn't all that different," said Sandra. "We have people cooking our food, cleaning our apartments, and entertaining us with music and educational programs. And we have the shuttle bus. We're living a fine lifestyle."

"I guess you're right," Barbara said with a laugh. "When you put it that way, I can see what you mean. But I will say I'd sure love a ride in one of those carriages."

The four entered the ballroom ready for the distraction of a lovely musical interlude. The string quartet was a welcome relief from the tension of the past two days, and the women drifted into another world as they relaxed in their seats. The quartet began with Mozart and Haydn and then launched into a piece by Ravel. They ended with a strange, spritely piece by Prokofiev followed by enthusiastic applause. The musical diversion served as a pleasant interlude for the Tuesday Table Ladies. The mystery of Laura and her possible whereabouts would wait another day.

When Sandra got home about nine, she was surprised to find a message from Robert asking her to call him. She pushed the callback button. She was eager to share what they had learned on the computer about Uncle Bud.

"Oh Robert, I know you're anxious to hear what we found out. We know his name and the firm's name and that he remarried, but not to Laura, to a woman named Sylvia, and they live in Philadelphia. So Laura's surely not involved with them at all." Sandra was racing. "So we've decided to put our investigation on hold since we keep running into dead ends everywhere. Maybe she just went on a little trip and forgot to tell—"

"Hold on, Sandra, not so fast! Take a deep breath. Your information is very interesting, but I was calling because something else has come up. I'm afraid Laura might actually be in danger."

"Oh no!"

"Can you get the group together in the usual place by ten tomorrow morning? I need to talk to all of you. There's nothing we can do tonight. It'll wait until morning."

Sandra agreed. She hung up. *What could have happened since yesterday to change Robert's mind about Laura's disappearance? If he's as alarmed as he sounded, he must have heard something bad.* She grimly picked up the phone to make arrangements for the meeting.

CHAPTER NINE

A Strange Coincidence

There is no friend like an old friend who has shared our morning days, no greeting like his welcome, no homage like his praise.
—OLIVER WENDELL HOLMES SR.

A fter Robert had left the women on Thursday morning to continue the search on their own, he felt he had done all he could to help them. The new computer search they were to undertake might be useful as might inquiries at the beauty salon at putting their minds at rest. He picked up his newspaper, having decided to get on with other things. He thought those energetic and shrewd women were perfectly capable of following the few leads they had. He admired their affection and concern for Laura, who it seemed had not let them get too close to her. It was unlikely there was cause for real concern. In the event that they became overzealous in their search, Harriet would make sure that they were kept within reasonable bounds in their investigations.

Despite himself, he had grown quite fond of them. They were making the most of the current stages of their lives. They were single; they looked out for each other almost as if they had been lifelong friends. He was a bit envious, he admitted. The single men at Oakwood seemed not to have formed comparable bonds. Perhaps it was because there were fewer of them and they seemed to have little in common. *Or is it because men are less willing to confide in each other?*

He knew of a foursome who played golf when the weather was good, but since the weather had turned, he had not seen them together. Of course there was the Tuesday evening men's table, but those who gathered there appeared to treat that more as a matter of convenience than of a place to develop friendships.

The women at Oakwood did indeed outnumber the men, but contrary to the jokes and myths about retirement communities, they did not chase after male companionship. There were of course married couples who were self-sufficient and often had social contacts with other couples. And not every couple was actually married. Robert did not concern himself with anyone's marital status given his own mother's escapades. Nonetheless, a few men had developed friendships with women; they could occasionally be seen dining or walking together around the grounds.

He would have thought the married couples were the lucky ones in such a setting, but he noticed that in some cases, one partner was frailer than the other and the stronger one often served as caregiver. He had once been told, "Old age ain't for sissies." He got off that gloomy train of thought with a reminder of the spirited Tuesday Table Ladies. Their motto seemed to be, as his twice-divorced grandmother had once told him, "There's many a good tune to be played on an old fiddle."

He hoped he could find contentment at Oakwood even if he felt cut off from the life he had led. He knew that the decision to go there was the best of all the alternatives and that he was lucky to be born in a country where such an option existed. After the dangers he had survived, he was lucky to be anywhere at all.

He was still feeling a bit solitary when his phone rang. *The ladies again? Can't be.* He felt he had been clear that he had ended his involvement. He picked up the phone expecting a robocall as usual.

"Hello, Rob! This is a voice from the past," said the caller confidently.

"Steve, I'd know your voice anywhere. Good to hear it. You old rascal, where are you?"

"Rob, I'm in your neck of the woods on assignment. I have a couple of hours free at noon. Can we meet? I'd love to catch up."

It was so good to hear from his former colleague. "You say where and I'll be there."

They agreed to meet at the Chesapeake Grill, which was convenient for Steve. Robert had been there and knew they didn't play the loud music the younger generations demanded these days if you could even call it music.

He was happy at the prospect of seeing Steve O'Malley again. Several years ago, they had worked together on a difficult case for the Department of State. A junior South American diplomat in New York had been suspected of smuggling looted gold treasures into the United States from an archaeological site in Peru; it was presumed to be Incan treasure destined for the underground art market.

There had been a dispute about whether the most-junior diplomats were covered by diplomatic immunity provisions, but that point became moot when the Peruvian government recalled the man and subsequently charged him with stealing national treasures. After that, Robert and Steve had kept in touch and had gotten together whenever they could.

Steve was often the FBI agent assigned to investigate cases of art contraband. He was in his fifties; while younger than Robert, they had formed a healthy respect for each other's expertise and dependability. Steve had been a champion wrestler in college, but his mother had been an artist and had influenced his decision to major in art history. His first job had been in an art-appraisal firm, but he had eventually opted for something more exciting. The FBI provided that excitement while making use of his art expertise.

After the usual warm handshakes and back-slapping typical of old friends meeting after a long absence, they were shown to a secluded booth next to a window. A cheerful waiter took their orders for beer. Steve was glad to see his old friend again. He had learned a lot from Robert's cultivated and tactful style. He had been impressed by his *savoir faire*, an expression he had picked up from Robert though he couldn't say it with a French accent like Robert's.

Steve was a muscular diamond in the rough who was fearless in any situation. His presence in pursuit of criminals would in his own words scare the knickers off a frog. A study in contrasts, the two men admired and trusted each other.

"You're looking good, Rob. Retirement must suit you."

Robert responded with a rueful smile. "I'm doing okay, Steve, but there are times when I miss the old life."

Steve understood. He could not imagine retiring himself. "I saw you drive up in that classy Jaguar you inherited from your mom." Steve was driving a government-issued black Ford.

Robert grinned. "The Jag is one great car, Steve. For Mom, it was an image builder. For me, it means speed. But tell me, how are things with you? What brings you here?"

"Things are fine. I'm still living with Lindsey, and I'm here for the usual reason. I'm on the trail of stolen art. Let's order lunch. I'll fill you in."

They motioned their waiter over. Steve ordered steak and fries and Robert chose crab cakes, a regional specialty.

"You may have read in the local papers that a man was found critically wounded two days ago in a DC park. He was taken to a hospital not too far from here. He's still unconscious and under police protection. He'd been stabbed. He's not expected to survive."

"What does this have to do with you, Steve?"

"The police think he's Italian based on a letter they found in his pocket. He was wearing some kind of religious medallion with his name engraved. We checked him out. Same name as a race car driver who was well-known years ago. CIA says a man of that name had been suspected of helping transport stolen art in Europe. Nothing was ever proven at the time. Once again, I'm working with the CIA in the hopes that he recovers consciousness and can tell us what happened."

Robert was listening intently.

Steve continued. "I've been briefed about the background to all this. It's a strange case. His money wasn't taken, so robbery doesn't seem to have been the motive. The hospital will call me if and when he regains consciousness and is able to talk."

Their meals came. They started to eat. "The call could come anytime, so I better be ready," said Steve between mouthfuls.

"What's the name of this poor guy, Steve?"

Steve paused to chew and swallow a mouthful. "Eduardo Giotti."

Robert thought carefully. It was a strange coincidence but not an impossible one. He had just spoken to Eduardo on Sunday. *Perhaps this is related to Laura's disappearance.* He would need to know more.

As the waiter approached to clear their plates and offer dessert, Steve's phone rang. Before Robert could say anything, Steve got the news that the doctors had said that there were early signs of regaining consciousness. He had to return at once to the hospital and stand by.

"I'd like to come with you, Steve. I think this is someone I know. I ran into him in Washington on Sunday."

Steve scarcely showed he was surprised by this unexpected revelation. In his work, he had experienced many strange coincidences. "In that case, you'd better come." They paid the bill and hastily made for the parking lot. "Rob, I'm on duty. Shucks, we'll have to go in the old Ford."

But Robert drove his own car and followed Steve to the hospital. On the way up to the private room where Eduardo Giotti was lying, he told Steve that, when posted to Rome in his early career, he had met Eduardo. But before he could explain further, they reached the hospital room.

"Perhaps you could identify him for us." Steve was hopeful. "We're pretty sure it's the same man, but this would clinch it."

Steve identified himself to the guard outside the room and introduced Robert, who had an ID as a former State Department officer to satisfy the guard. They were disappointed; the injured man had an oxygen mask over his nose and mouth and a bandage around his head. He was hooked up to a tangle of IVs and machines monitoring his vitals. There was no way Robert could possibly ID him as the smart, well-groomed man he had seen in Washington even though that had been so recently. Robert shook his head.

His eyes fell on a scrap of crumpled paper lying on Eduardo's bloodstained clothes that were in a heap on a chair. Robert carefully picked the paper up to hand to Steve but not before he glanced at its contents. The attending nurse noted his interest and told him she had found the paper so tightly held in the patient's hand when he had been brought in that the police must have missed it.

The injured man began to moan. His eyelids fluttered. The machine monitoring the vitals signaled an emergency. The nurse hit a button to summon help.

"I'll get out of the way, Steve. Let me know what happens, and I'll fill you in on what I know about him."

"I'll call you at home."

On the way out, Robert bought a large cup of strong coffee in the hospital lobby and made his way back to Oakwood with a heavy heart and many questions. *Could this be related to Laura's absence?* He realized he would have to share this development with the Tuesday Table Ladies, but he decided to do that only after he had gotten an update from Steve.

CHAPTER TEN

An Iconic Puzzle

The aim of art is to represent not the outward appearance of things but their inward significance.

—ARISTOTLE

D uring the long drive back to Oakwood, Robert reviewed the events of the day. Eduardo had been urgently trying to meet with Laura, but he was close to death and she had disappeared. It had been great to see Steve again but a surprise to find him involved in a case that might be relevant to Laura's whereabouts. It had been as great a surprise for Steve that Robert told him he had known a race car driver named Eduardo years earlier in Rome and of his recent encounter with Eduardo in Washington.

His thoughts returned to that scrap of paper. He had noted three barely legible letters before handing it to Steve; they had been written in pencil with a shaky hand. He couldn't be sure, but they looked like an *i*, a *c*, and an *o*. He said them aloud. *What could they mean? What was Eduardo trying to say? Why were these three letters so important to him even when he was so badly injured?* He was mulling these questions as he reached his cottage.

He had barely entered when the phone rang. It was Steve. "We've lost him I'm afraid. He muttered a few words just before he died, but he was so agitated and talking so fast that I couldn't understand him with my very limited Italian. The only word I could make out was 'econa' or something like that. The rest was unintelligible."

Before Robert could reply, Steve said, "Have to run, Robert. I'm on my way to Italy to follow another lead on the smuggling case. The DC cops will be handling the murder investigation anyway. We have a positive match on the fingerprints, so we won't need you to ID him. He was Eddie Giotti, as we thought."

"Steve, before you go, let me ask you one thing. What makes you think Eduardo was involved in art smuggling?"

"We had a tip that several years ago, a gang was using European race car drivers to smuggle art objects. Apparently, they hid them in their race cars, which were towed all over Europe. The race cars were seldom searched at the borders. Eduardo is just one of a number of retired drivers we're looking at. Sorry, I have to go Robert. My plane's boarding. Great seeing you. We'll keep in touch."

"That we will," Robert replied. "Have a good flight."

He poured himself a large brandy and settled down in his comfortable easy chair to contemplate the puzzle. Robert thoughtfully considered what Steve had just told him. *So Eduardo's gone. Had he met with Laura before he was killed? Could she be involved in his death in any way? And what did he try to tell the police? Did Eduardo know where he was and who he was speaking to, or was he just delirious?*

There was no solid evidence to tie Eduardo's murder to Laura's absence, but he had called her the day that she disappeared, pleading with her to meet him, and then he was killed some time later that same day. Too many coincidences. As Robert mulled over the possibilities, he felt the need for a long walk in the crisp fall night air to clear his head. Walking always helped him think. The movement of his body seemed to stimulate his brain cells. He grabbed a jacket and headed out.

He walked along the riverbank. His thoughts returned to the scrap of paper. *What was he trying to say with his final words? I. C. O. And then he said something like "econa" in the hospital. Could that have been "icona," Italian for icon? Could an icon have been part of the smuggled artwork Steve's investigating? Had Eduardo been trying to tell anyone at all where the stolen art was hidden?* Steve hadn't told him what kinds of art they were looking for, but Robert knew that some icons could be quite valuable and thus certainly worth stealing. He stopped. *Of course. Laura's apartment. She has one hanging in her living room.* He shivered, but not because of the cold. He realized the icon could have been the connection between Laura's disappearance and Eduardo's death. Too many coincidences.

He wished he'd had an opportunity to discuss this in depth with Steve. He had wanted to talk to him more about it in the hospital, but things there had moved too fast. He assumed they would have had a chance to get together when Steve left the hospital. He wanted time to talk with Steve in detail about Laura and her past and present connection to Eduardo. That was something to be discussed in person, not over the phone or in emails. His years with the State Department had trained him to be cautious when using an unsecured phone. He could have used Steve's expertise in stolen art and perhaps have even shown him Laura's icon, but for the time being, Steve was flying over the Atlantic and Robert was on his own.

Robert remembered Laura's icon had some cracks along the edge as though it might have been quite old. He wondered if Laura might have had it repaired at some point. If it were as old as it looked, it might have been quite valuable and could indeed have been part of the stolen art works Steve was concerned about. If it had been repaired locally, it might have also been appraised for insurance purposes. He could think of no way to get such information from the insurance company even if he knew which one it was, but he figured he just might be able to discover which dealer had repaired it and had perhaps appraised it.

He had become sufficiently facile at searching the Internet at least for basic information. "You would be wise, Robert, to take a course in technology before you graduate," old Dr. Yeats had said. "It's the next big thing coming down the pike, and if you don't get into it now, you may regret it later on." He fired up his laptop and googled "icon," "repair," "art, "restoration," "Maryland," and "DC," casting a broad net to begin with. If Laura had taken the icon to be repaired after she had moved to Oakwood, there might be a record of it. In any case, an art restoration expert might be knowledgeable about the value of early icons. They would certainly know a lot more than he did.

He scoured all the hits that popped up. Way at the top was Jones and Longwell Restorations in Bethesda, Maryland. He had to dig for the phone number, way down at the bottom of the webpage, but he found it and dialed it. The man who answered seemed annoyed by Robert's generalized question about the restoration of icons. "Sir, it would all depend on the value of the object, which would be determined by its provenance as well as the hours of work or research involved in restoring it."

"Have you repaired any icons from the twelfth or thirteenth centuries?"

The man on the phone became instantaneously courteous. "Why yes! My partner in New York is an expert in such antiquities. He engages in restorations for museums, galleries, law firms handling estates that include such art, and private collections. What might you be interested in having restored?"

"It's an old icon that belongs to a friend of mine. Have you done any restoration work in the DC area with antique icons?"

"Not here, but as I mentioned, I work closely with a colleague in New York who has had extensive experience with them. He is very highly regarded in the United States and in Europe for his knowledge of icons, Byzantine, Russian, and Orthodox, and I am sure we can help your friend."

"Thank you very much for your time. I'll give her your name and phone number, and she'll be in touch with you."

"Oh please do keep us in mind," the voice on the phone urged in an unctuous tone.

Robert assured him he would do that in an equally unctuous tone.

So, it seemed Laura had not taken the icon to them for restoration. Since that conversation had led nowhere, he decided that he should let the women know what had happened. Perhaps they knew something about Laura's icon; she may have mentioned it to one of them and even said where she had gotten it. He would ask them to return to Laura's apartment with him to examine it more closely. Perhaps it had some markings on the back. He hoped that it might even have a sales tag proving it was not related to Eduardo and the stolen art. He needed another look at that icon.

He particularly wanted to talk to Ellen and Sandra to see what they might find on the computer concerning stolen art and icons. Fortunately, Ellen and Sandra were highly skilled and should be able to find something about lost or stolen European art, he thought. He hoped that they could learn more about how stolen art was disposed of, as well as about the black market in icons.

It was 7:30 when Robert dialed Sandra. He was disappointed when she didn't answer, but he left a message and settled back in his chair to read the newspaper. It had been a very eventful day.

CHAPTER ELEVEN

Troubling News

Murder most foul.

—WILLIAM SHAKESPEARE

W hen Robert walked into the activity room the following morning, the five women were at the table anxiously waiting to hear what he had to say.

"Good morning, and thanks for coming. I asked to meet with you because something has happened that may have a bearing on Laura's disappearance." He paused to gather his thoughts before continuing. He pulled a folded newspaper clipping from his pocket and handed it to Harriet. "This was on the back page of this morning's *Washington Post*. I think it will show you why we may have cause to be concerned about Laura. Would you read it out loud to the others?"

Harriet did. "Stabbing Victim Dies. An elderly man found unconscious in a city park on Tuesday evening died of multiple stab wounds yesterday without regaining consciousness. Police have identified him as Eduardo Giotti, an Italian citizen who had flown into Dulles Airport from Rome last week. Records indicate that he had once been an internationally celebrated race car driver who was known as Eddie G and who was frequently in the newspapers for his dramatic actions on and off the race track. He had faded from the headlines in recent years and was reportedly living quietly outside Rome. Police reported that they have no leads at the moment."

Harriet looked at Robert in consternation. "What does this mean? Who is this? Why are you showing this to us? Could he be the man who left the message for Laura on the answering machine?"

"I'm afraid he is," replied Robert. "Eduardo was an old friend of Laura's. I met them both in Rome many years ago and was surprised to run into him in the lobby of the Mayflower Hotel in Washington last Sunday. He seemed somewhat agitated. He said it was urgent that he talk to Laura as soon as possible. He had written to her but hadn't gotten an answer. I told him she had mentioned getting his letter but seemed reluctant to talk to him. He said he was going to call her and wanted me to speak to her again, but I told him I didn't want to get involved. Now I wish I had. He might still be alive."

"Oh my God," exclaimed Ellen. "Stabbed to death. I knew there was something scary about him when we heard that voice on the phone."

"I thought he sounded more anxious than scary," Barbara said.

"Why didn't you tell us then that you knew him?" Karen asked. "We all wondered later if you were the Roberto he referred to." She tried to keep the annoyance from her voice.

"At that point, I wasn't at all convinced that his call was related to your concerns about Laura. Now, it looks as if I might have been wrong."

Barbara looked at the clipping. "This says he was stabbed on Tuesday. That's the day he left the message on Laura's machine. Maybe she returned his call and arranged to meet him. If she had done that, she might have been in danger too."

The other women murmured and looked at each other in astonishment. Though they had read many mystery stories, this was the closest any of them had come to an actual murder.

"His death may have nothing to do with Laura," Harriet pointed out with her usual skepticism.

"He may have been a random victim of some thug roaming the park."

"It's certainly something to worry about," Barbara said. "There are too many coincidences here. Eduardo calls her on Tuesday hoping to meet her somewhere, and then he's killed and Laura disappears. As a lawyer, I learned to be suspicious of too many coincidences. It just doesn't add up."

"And from what Patti says, she was planning on meeting someone," Karen said.

"Eddie G," murmured Sandra, who had been quiet. "I saw him race one time in Monaco."

"What? Did you? I can't believe it!" Ellen said while the others looked at Sandra wide-eyed.

"Yes. I haven't thought about that in years," Sandra said slowly. "I was in Europe on vacation with some friends, and while we were in Monaco, we heard about a big, exciting race, so we decided to go. It must have been over fifty years ago, in the early sixties. Eddie G was still winning a lot of races and was frequently in the headlines with one beautiful model or another. We went partly just to see him."

Sandra's memories flooded back. "He was something to see even then—very handsome, wavy black hair, strutting around in a red driving outfit, playing to the crowd. He was something all right. I would've run off with him in a minute!"

Just as Laura did, thought Robert. "Yet another coincidence," he said. "What are the chances of finding a woman in a retirement community who had seen a certain Italian race car driver fifty years before?"

"We had past lives too!" Sandra said teasingly. "You aren't the only one here with an interesting history."

The other women nodded and smiled.

"What can we do now?" asked Ellen, quickly getting back to the topic. "We must find Laura soon. Perhaps we should go to the police."

"I've given that a lot of thought," Robert replied. "But there's one more thing you should know. I had lunch yesterday with an old friend who was in Washington to investigate an international art smuggling operation. He seemed to think Eduardo might have been involved. When my friend Steve found out that I knew Eduardo, he took me along to the hospital hoping I could identify him."

The women stared at him in astonishment.

"You actually went to the hospital to see this Eduardo?" asked Ellen. "What happened?"

"Well, he was so heavily bandaged and I had so little contact with him that I couldn't be much help. But while I was there, I happened to see a scrap of paper on which Eduardo had written what looked like three letters, *i, c,* and *o,* and I wondered about it. The writing was very faint and almost illegible, so I couldn't be sure.

"Then my friend called before he left town last night to tell me that just before Eduardo died, he kept repeating something that sounded like *econa,* which I realized could have been *icona,* Italian for icon. That word, along with the letters on the paper, led me to wonder whether his killers were after an icon they believed Eduardo had taken. That reminded me of the antique icon in Laura's living room. I can't help wondering if there's a connection and if that's why Eduardo wanted to talk to Laura. Do any of you know anything about the icon? Where she got it and when?"

Barbara replied, "I asked her about it once, and she mentioned it had been given to her by an old friend years ago and had a lot of sentimental value."

"We still don't have much to go on," Robert said. "It's only a tenuous connection at best. We don't want to embarrass Laura if her disappearance is unrelated to Eduardo's death. And we certainly don't want to involve Oakwood in a murder unless it's absolutely necessary. I can envision the headlines that would cause. Why don't I speak to Cathy and fill her in on this? It's her call at this point. When I spoke to her before, she was very reluctant to involve the authorities, especially since Laura had left a sign-out sheet."

The women turned expectantly to Harriet. She sighed and reluctantly explained to Robert that she had filled out the sign-out sheet and put it onto the front desk so the others would calm down until Laura returned on her own. "I realize I probably shouldn't have done that, but at the time, I thought they were making a big deal out of nothing. Now I know how wrong I was."

Robert seemed quite taken aback by this revelation but responded in his usual diplomatic manner. "I can understand your thinking, but I'm afraid it may have misled us. I'll have to let Cathy know about that."

"There are a couple of other things we wanted to tell you," Sandra said. "As you suggested, we talked to Laura's hairdresser, Patti, and she indicated that Laura was apparently going to meet someone. Furthermore, we found out that Laura's car isn't in any of the parking lots at Oakwood, so it looks as though she left voluntarily."

"I guess I was wrong when I said we had a mystery but no crime," said Harriet. "Now we have both a crime and a mystery, but we still don't know if they're related."

"That's right," Robert said. "And let's not tie the crime to Oakwood if we can help it. We certainly don't want the national press camped on the lawn of our quiet community of retirees. We'd better keep all this to ourselves for now."

"Is there anything at all we can do at this point?" asked Barbara. "I hate just sitting around hoping Laura will turn up on her own."

"Yes, I feel so helpless," Karen said. Helpless was the last word Karen would normally use to describe herself. She was a woman of action who was always so sure of herself, but she had to admit these were humbling circumstances.

"I think there are a couple of things we might do," Robert said. "Perhaps we could get a closer look at that icon in Laura's apartment. Would one or two of you be willing to go with me this afternoon to take another look around?"

"Sure," said Karen. "I have the key. We can take as much time as you need."

"And hope she doesn't come back while you're snooping," Harriet interjected.

"Anyone know anything about icons?" Robert asked, looking around the group.

"The only icons I know about are the little images on my computer screen, but I take it you're talking about some sort of painting," Ellen said.

"I know a little bit. I was an art history major in college," Barbara said.

The others looked at her in surprise.

"I thought you were a lawyer," Sandra said.

"When I finished college, law looked like a better career path. There weren't too many museums crying for art historians at the time, and running an art gallery didn't appeal to me. Even if I'd gotten a graduate degree, there was no guarantee of a job. Women were just getting into law at that time, and women lawyers became very marketable. Besides, the law appealed to me. I like the logical arguments the legal process requires."

"Barbara, would you be willing to go to Laura's apartment with Karen this afternoon and take a look at the icon?" asked Robert. "I'll join you there."

"I'll be glad to do anything that helps us find Laura. I'm more worried than ever now that we know there's been a murder."

"One other thing we haven't talked about," Robert said. "When I inquired at the lobby desk, John said that Laura had had an outside call Tuesday morning from a woman who knew where Laura lived but didn't have her phone number. It's possible that she might have gone to meet this woman rather than Eduardo. Does anyone know who that might be?"

The women shook their heads. "I can't think of anyone, but then, we don't know a lot about her friends," said Sandra.

"Of course she might have done something else entirely," Robert replied.

"Yes. I still think we're speculating without much evidence to go on," said Harriet. "I'm afraid that she'll get angry at us for prying into her personal life for little or no reason. After all, she could walk in here at any moment."

The other women looked around uneasily.

"You're right we don't have much to go on, but Eduardo's death certainly puts a more somber light on it," Karen said.

"I wish there was more we could do," said Sandra.

"Perhaps there is," Robert replied. "I was wondering if you and Ellen might want to do some Internet research on stolen antique icons and see what you can dig up that might be helpful. This art smuggling business reminds me of the stories about stolen art works during the Second World War. There could be a connection."

"Sure!" Ellen said. "I'll be glad to do something besides worrying. I can easily change my plans for today. How about you, Sandy?"

"That's fine with me. I'll bring my laptop over right after lunch."

"Good. That's settled. I'd better speak to Cathy. I'll meet you two at one o'clock at Laura's apartment," Robert said, looking at Karen and Barbara.

The women rose, still absorbing the fact that a murder had occurred and that they had all heard the victim's voice on the day he had been killed. Sandra was lost in thought about the young Eddie G, whom she had found so attractive. The whole situation seemed unreal in the peaceful environs of Oakwood. But at least they felt there were things they could do.

Robert headed for Cathy's office and stuck his head in the door. She was on the phone but motioned for him to have a seat while she finished her conversation. He stepped into the room, quietly closed the door, and sat in the chair across from her desk.

"What's up?" asked Cathy as she hung up.

"I think you should know about some new developments in this situation with Laura. Remember I told you about the brief marriage between Laura and Eduardo?" He handed her the clipping from the *Washington Post*. "This is Eddie. An old friend who is still with the government took me to see him in the hospital yesterday, hoping I could identify him, but he was so bandaged that I couldn't get a good look. They did get a fingerprint match, so my ID wasn't needed. My friend's back in Europe by now, investigating an art smuggling ring he thinks Eduardo might have been involved in."

"Do you think this has anything to do with Laura's disappearance?" asked Cathy.

"There's a possible tie-in with Laura."

Robert explained his hypothesis about Laura's icon and its possible relevance to Eduardo's murder. "Two of the women are going back into her apartment to take another look at that icon. I'll go with them. Karen Brown has a key, so I hope that gives us some legal cover if a question ever arises, but I thought I should let you know."

"Thanks. I hope nothing has happened to Laura, but I'm also worried about this involving Oakwood in a scandal. We don't need that."

"There's something else you need to know. Apparently, Laura didn't leave a sign-out sheet after all. One of the women confessed to signing Laura out because she thought the others were overreacting. She thought that if it looked as though Laura had signed out, they'd drop all their worrying about it. Then on the other hand, your tip about the hairdresser paid off. It seems Laura told Patti she was meeting someone, though we don't know who. Also, her car's gone, so it looks as if she left on her own."

"Let's hope she wasn't going to meet this Eduardo character," replied Cathy.

"I've told the group we don't have enough to go to the police with at this point, and they're satisfied with that. I assume you still agree."

"Oh yes. What would we tell them? She's gone away and didn't tell her friends where she was going? Even so, the connection to Eduardo is disturbing, and if the newspapers got hold of it, Oakwood would be on the front page with all sorts of wild rumors."

"You're right. We should definitely keep this quiet until we have more to go on. I'll keep you posted if anything new turns up. By the way, the women found out that Nora's Uncle Bud had had his marriage derailed by someone other than Laura, so Nora was way off track. I'm thinking about how best to get back to her. I'll let you know."

"It sounds like these women have been busy with their investigations," Cathy said. "Let me know if you find anything else. This whole affair is becoming worrisome."

CHAPTER TWELVE
Augusta Cleans

If you obey all the rules, you miss all the fun.
—KATHERINE HEPBURN

R obert returned to his apartment frustrated, annoyed, and worried. He was at a loss about how to proceed. Cathy had agreed that it was pointless to go to the police. There was too little to go on; all was conjecture and circumstance. He was irritated that the women had gotten him into this predicament. He had always had confidence in his judgment, but then, he had had all the resources of his government behind him. This time, he was on his own. Steve was on his way to Rome. Meanwhile, he envisioned Laura, having a happy time, oblivious of the consternation she had left behind. He was annoyed with her too. His mood was uncharacteristic. *Robert, you're becoming a cantankerous old man. Face it. You're growing old.*

He did battle with those thoughts. *Get hold of yourself! You've dealt with many infinitely worse situations. This one is child's play by comparison.* It worried him nonetheless; he was indeed growing old.

He decided to spend the next half hour in the exercise room to get some of his endorphins working to dispel his mood. Then he would return to tidy up his papers before his housekeeper, Augusta, arrived to clean his cottage.

❧

Augusta was fiendishly diligent in her work. She drove her cleaning cart with its broom rampant like a flag as if off to war. Indeed, she had triumphed over many a dusty foe in the often-overstuffed rooms of the residences. Although not so young herself, her brisk and ruthless approach would have struck fear in the hearts of the dear old ladies and gents but for the surprisingly gentle way she talked to them.

Augusta had grown fond of them, and they in turn opened their hearts to her and told her their life stories. She especially liked Mrs. Brown; Sandra made her smile. She knew Mrs. Brown was one of the women who met for dinner every Tuesday, and

Mrs. Brown was her favorite. She was full of stories, some of which had shocked her at first, but they made her realize what a happy but sheltered life she herself had led.

Mrs. Brown had even confided in her that she had had a face-lift. Augusta had seen a program about cosmetic face-lifts and understood the risks. But Mrs. Brown had told her "Oh! Augusta, lots of women have face-lifts these days. Since they discovered penicillin, it's no longer dangerous." Augusta knew she herself would never have one. *Why, that would cost a fortune!* But she knew why Mrs. Brown had one. *She likes men, and men like her.*

Once when she was doing the annual spring clean for Mrs. Brown, she saw an open photo album on the bedroom table. There were pictures of a younger-looking Sandra with different good-looking men. Augusta was amazed. *Where did she find them all?* When Mrs. Brown saw her looking at the pictures, she simply remarked with a wink, "It was never with married men." Augusta hoped that was true.

Augusta arrived fully armed to tackle Robert's cottage. "Sorry I'm late, Mr. Symonds. It took me a bit longer than I thought it would to clean Mrs. Lambert's apartment. I don't think Nora was as fussy as me tho' she always seemed busy. I tell you, Mr. Symonds, it reminded me of my mother, who didn't like cleaning very much. She used to spray the air with lemon polish just before my dad came home to make him think she'd been cleaning all day while he was at work; actually, she had been enjoying her soaps."

Augusta donned her rubber gloves and went to work. While dusting the sitting room she asked, "Do you know when Mrs. Lambert will be back? I just cleaned her place for the first time and I found two letters between the chair cushions. I thought they might be important, so I left them on the side table for her."

Robert was only half listening. Back from his workout in the exercise room, his mind was far away, reflecting on the recent events and what he had told Cathy. He made a ham sandwich when Augusta left the coast clear in the kitchen. He was used to making his own lunch most days; he found lunch at the Oakwood café uninteresting. He was not, as he had found out, a mac-and-cheese guy.

Augusta had the vacuum cleaner on full throttle. Time for Robert to retreat. It was approaching one o'clock. He made his way to his meeting with Barbara and Karen.

On his way to Laura's apartment, he passed the large picture window that overlooked the river. The signs of late autumn foretold the coming of winter. He would have to decide soon whether to stay holed up at Oakwood or make arrangements to head south with the rest of the snow birds. He had heard that Oakwood, festive with lights and decorated trees, was delightful at Christmas time. And then there were those parties in Washington not that far away. *Perhaps I should stay here at least until after the holidays.*

Barbara and Karen were waiting for him in Laura's apartment. He and Barbara went directly to the small icon in the niche on the far wall.

"I never looked at it before," said Barbara. "There are so many interesting works of art in this room."

"Yes. It would be easy to overlook this one," Robert said.

"Can we take it over to the window so we can see it in the light?" Barbara asked.

"Sure." Robert retrieved a pair of cotton gloves from his pocket. He lifted the icon out of the niche and carefully laid it on the end table under the window.

They examined the icon closely, the gold halo still shining through centuries of dust. The image, which was about eight by ten inches, was a traditional Madonna holding a child in front of two angels hovering over her shoulders.

"I'm certainly no expert on icons," Barbara said, "but this is obviously not encaustic. It looks like tempera on a wood panel, a common medium. Encaustic was rarely used after the iconoclastic period, although it has made a comeback in recent years." Seeing Robert's puzzled look, she said, "Many early icons were painted with melted beeswax mixed with colored pigments. Let's look at the back." Robert gently turned over the icon; they examined the back of the wooden panel.

"They were always concerned that the painting would be cracked if the panel warped, so they sometimes used wooden strips like these as braces to keep it flat. It looks like a couple of these strips are new. She must have had it repaired fairly recently."

"Can you tell how old it is?" asked Robert.

"No. It would take an expert to analyze the varnish and other materials to determine that. I can't even tell you if it's Byzantine or Russian. All I can say for sure is that it might be quite old, possibly fourteenth or even thirteenth century, but it could be much later. Art historians have never known quite what to do with icons. They don't fit neatly into categories of Western art. However, artists are making excellent copies today. There are plenty for sale on eBay, so we'd need a competent appraiser to place a date and value on this one. But it's possible that this is quite valuable."

Robert replaced the icon in the niche and removed his gloves.

Karen had been walking around the room looking at the objects on the walls. "I've probably been in this room a dozen times but have never been observant," she said. "Look at this old photograph." She pointed to a framed black-and-white photo of a stone farmhouse with black shutters and surrounded by trees. "I wonder where that house is. It's so plain and ordinary. It looks like a candidate for a house makeover on HGTV. I wonder why she has that photo hanging here."

Barbara peered at it. "I have no idea. I've never noticed it before, though it's probably been hanging here all along. Laura never mentioned it. It must have some special meaning for her."

As they turned to leave, Barbara noticed the opened envelopes on the side table. "Hey! Where did these come from? They weren't here when I was in here before."

"Augusta mentioned something about finding some letters this morning when she cleaned here," Robert said. "She told me that when she was cleaning my place."

Barbara picked up one. "Postmarked in Washington last week," she commented as she pulled out a single sheet of paper and read it aloud. "Carissima Laura, I told you in my letter last month that I would be coming to America soon to meet with you. Since you did not answer, I hope that you received my letter. Now I am here in Washington and hope we can see each other as soon as possible. I would really like to get the present I gave you so long ago and want to explain in person why it is so important. I only hope that you still have it and that I will be able to return with it to Italy. I will be calling you in a day or two to arrange a time and place to meet. Eduardo."

"That must be the letter he mentioned to me," said Robert. "The one she was reluctant to talk about. I wonder if he could be referring to the icon.

Perhaps she didn't want to give it back, and that's why she wouldn't return his calls."

They turned their attention to the other letter addressed to "Mrs. Lambert." There was no return address on the envelope, but it had a California postmark and was dated the previous month. Barbara read it aloud. "I know you have been trying to reach me. I will be in touch with you soon. We must meet! Melissa."

"I wonder who that is and if they've met," Karen said.

"Another mystery," Barbara said as they left the apartment.

❦

Sandra arrived at Ellen's apartment carrying her laptop. "So what are we looking for?" Ellen asked.

"Anything that might connect the icon and stolen art work," answered Sandra. "Maybe one of us could search for stolen art and the other one could do a search on icons."

"I'd like to do icons because I don't know anything about them."

"Okay, let's get going. I'll set up on this table while you work at the desk. We'll print out anything that looks useful."

Having determined that Sandra's laptop already had the appropriate drive for Ellen's printer, they set to work.

"Gosh!" exclaimed Sandra after a few minutes. "I had no idea there were so many websites for stolen artwork. The FBI has one, Interpol has one, some of the museums have them, and there are some businesses that search for stolen works. I didn't realize that stolen art was such a big business."

"I always think of the Nazi art thefts during World War II," said Ellen. "Apparently, Hitler wanted to have a museum that held the greatest art in the world, and his thugs went around Europe stealing works of art. Did you see that movie about the artwork stolen during the war? A lot of the art was never returned to the owners. Of course, many of them were dead by the time the art was recovered, and some of it is in private collections or museums today."

The two worked quietly, searching through numerous websites, looking for anything that might be relevant.

Ellen broke the silence. "Hey Sandy, did you know that the word *iconoclast* initially referred to religious leaders who banned the use of icons? They felt that icons were sacrilegious and destroyed most of the early Byzantine icons. There are a few left. Seems the British Museum has several, but they are extremely rare, so I don't think Laura's could be one of the very early ones. But icons became very popular again in the twelfth and thirteenth centuries, and they're still being made today."

"I thought most of them were in churches."

"Yes, they're often made for churches, but also for private homes. They are frequently handed down from generation to generation. Some are 'praying icons' that inspire people in prayer. There are dozens of books on icons. Who knew they were so popular?"

The two women spent the next few hours perusing websites for any information about icons and stolen art that might have a connection to Eduardo's death and possibly to Laura. As expected, there was nothing about the FBI investigation of stolen artwork smuggled by European race car drivers. That case was still under investigation and had not been made public, even after all these years. Occasionally, one of the women printed out a few pages of material she thought might be important. They stopped for coffee and discussed what they had found.

"I don't know that we can go any further without knowing more about Laura's particular icon," Ellen said. "We have a lot of background info that might be helpful, but now we need to talk to the others and see what they've found out."

"I guess I had better make another dinner reservation at Riverview," Sandra said. "I'll invite Robert too."

"I'll call the others and let them know," said Ellen.

CHAPTER THIRTEEN
Dilemma

Falling down is part of life.
Getting back up is living.
—ANONYMOUS

H arriet was in her usual spot before the others arrived at Riverview. Ellen had called everyone, and Harriet had agreed to another meal with the Tuesday dinner group. She usually had Friday dinners with her speakers-series committee members along with the speaker for the evening's lecture. However, no lecture had been scheduled for that night, so she was able to make her excuses to the committee and join Ellen and the others for dinner.

She had spent a busy afternoon writing and distributing minutes for another of her committees as well as trying to line up interesting speakers for the following month. She was definitely ready to relax with friends and a glass of Pinot Grigio. She hoped there would be no more upsetting news that night. *Perhaps Laura will walk right in and put a stop to all this nonsense.* She looked around the room and wondered if some of the other residents had noticed the frequent meetings of the Tuesday group lately. While none of her committee members had said anything to her, a couple of them had looked a little strange when she told them she could not eat with them that night.

She was soon joined by Barbara and Sandra, who were also ready to relax after their busy afternoon. Robert arrived shortly afterward, and then Ellen and Karen came.

"Our dinner table's just not the same without Laura," remarked Barbara. "Though she never talks much about her own life, she's always so vibrant and full of fun and interested in everyone else. I miss her at our dinners."

"Yes, she's always fun to talk to. Our dinners have been much more somber without her," Ellen said. "Of course that's partly because we're all so worried about what might have happened to her. It's hard to be cheerful when a good friend has just disappeared."

Emily appeared with the menus and distributed wine glasses. The Friday night special was prime rib, which was usually cooked to perfection, so everyone except Ellen ordered it. Though she was not a strict vegetarian, she tried to limit her intake of meat. She opted for the flounder stuffed with Maryland crabmeat. While the others went to the salad bar, Robert and Barbara selected the marinated mushroom salad from the menu.

"Well," Sandra began when everyone was seated, "I thought we should get together and share information and see where we are. I don't know where we should go from here."

"I agree," Barbara replied. "Laura has been missing for four days, and we don't seem to be any closer to finding her than we were Tuesday night."

"It seems to be getting even more confusing and scary," Ellen said.

"I still think we may be getting ahead of ourselves," Harriet said. "I'm not convinced she's really missing just because we don't know where she is. What did you all find out today?"

Sandra spoke first. "Ellen and I did some research on stolen art, especially icons. We found there's an awful lot of stolen art floating around out there and a number of businesses and government organizations trying to track it all down." She briefly described what they had learned about icons and their history as well as some of the organizations that could be used to trace whether a piece of art had been stolen.

"We can't really say that this sheds any light on Laura's disappearance, but art theft is a serious matter, especially in Europe and the United States. The penalties can be very severe," Ellen said.

"We took another look at the icon in Laura's apartment and decided that it might be quite old and valuable, but it could have been painted much later," Barbara said. "Is it so valuable that art thieves would smuggle it across Europe? I don't know. There's no way to determine its real value without a professional appraisal."

"We also found a letter from Eduardo urging Laura to meet him so he could get back a gift he had given her years ago," Karen added. "We're guessing the icon might be what he was after. Maybe Laura's reluctance to meet with Eduardo was because he had given her the icon and she didn't want to return it to him."

"Why was Eduardo so desperate to get the gift back?" Sandra asked. "If it was the icon, did it have something to do with the stolen art work? And if so, were the art thieves threatening Eduardo unless he got it back and gave it to them?"

"Could Laura's icon even be the reason for Eduardo's murder?" Ellen's voice was shaky.

"We have many more questions than we have answers," Robert said. "Was Laura avoiding Eduardo because she didn't want to give back the icon? Or did she arrange to meet him after all? Could she have been involved in his killing in some way? Was she a target of the attack, along with Eduardo, and if so, has she been hurt or even killed?"

The women gasped as Robert put their worst fears into words. Even Harriet seemed upset at the possibility that Laura could have been in danger.

"If she didn't meet Eduardo," Robert said, "where did she go? And why hasn't she communicated with anyone here? Eduardo sounded quite desperate on the phone. If he was being threatened because Laura's icon was stolen and the thieves wanted it back, Laura could also be in serious danger. Is it possible she went into hiding to avoid the men who killed Eduardo?"

"What about the other letter we found?" Karen asked.

"Yes, that might be important," Robert said. "Apparently, Augusta, my housekeeper, has been assigned to Laura's apartment as Nora's replacement. She mentioned she'd found two letters that had slipped between the cushions of Laura's chair. We saw the letters on the table where Augusta had left them, and one, as we said, was from Eduardo. The other was addressed to Mrs. Lambert from someone named Melissa who also wanted to meet with Laura. Does anyone know who she might be?"

No one did.

"Where are the letters now?" asked Harriet.

"In Laura's apartment. We left them where we found them," Barbara replied.

"Even if Eduardo did want Laura to return the icon, it doesn't mean that the icon was stolen or that it had anything to do with his murder or her disappearance," Harriet pointed out.

"You're right," Robert said. "Though even the possibility of Laura's connection to the murder worries me. However, I'm reluctant to go to the police at this point. I spoke again to Cathy to let her know we'd be in Laura's apartment, and she still feels we have no real evidence to take to the police. We certainly don't want to drag Laura's name into the Eduardo investigation unless it's necessary. We just don't have enough to go on."

"We could contact one of the businesses that trace stolen art to see if her icon really was stolen," Ellen said.

"But what if they say it *was* stolen?" Barbara asked. "It's not ours. We can't do anything about it. We might be getting Laura into serious trouble with the authorities. Legally, she might be charged with possessing stolen goods even if she was unaware of its source."

"Again we come back to the same dilemma," Robert said with a sigh. "There's no clear path for us to take right now."

"I'm not sure we haven't already interfered in Laura's business more than we had any right to," said Harriet stiffly.

"But Harriet, she really could be in danger. There's already been one murder that we know of," Ellen said.

"We're back where we started," said Robert. "We know more than we did, but it doesn't seem to lead anywhere. We keep coming back to the same question, 'Where's Laura?'"

"Perhaps we're going at this from the wrong direction," said Sandra. "We keep starting at Oakwood and working outward. What if we start from a different perspective? Let's set aside all we've learned about Nora and Eduardo and icons. Where would Laura go? What places in her previous life might she go to? Whether she was running away from some art thieves or went off on a lark, where would she be likely to go? Back home to Boston? The Bahamas? Paris? Where would she run *to*?"

"Trouble is we don't know enough about her background to know where she might have gone. I know her mother's dead, but I think her father is still living. Does she have other relatives she might visit?" asked Ellen.

"What about in-laws? Does she have a relationship with them?" Harriet asked, getting into the discussion. This approach appealed to her more than snooping around Laura's apartment and speculating about stolen icons.

After several minutes of silence, Sandra said, "Just a minute. Come to think of it, isn't there some place up in Pennsylvania where Laura has visited? A place that's been in her family forever?"

Barbara put her fork down slowly. "Of course. You're right. I remember her talking about her grandfather's farm back in our DC days. She and her husband would occasionally go up there for a weekend. She said it wasn't anything fancy, just an old farmhouse that had been updated. No one was farming there anymore."

"Did you say farmhouse?" Karen asked. She turned to Barbara and Robert. "Remember that photograph on her wall? That must have some sentimental value for her to hang it next to her valuable paintings. I wonder if it could be a picture of her grandfather's house. There wasn't any writing on it, but mayb—"

"That's very possible," Barbara said. "Laura said her family had owned the land since William Penn decided to welcome people of all religions, not just Quakers, to their colony."

"Does anyone know where this house is?" asked Robert.

Ellen, who had sat quietly throughout the discussion, spoke up, shaking her head. "I've heard Laura mention that Pennsylvania place a couple of times, but I don't know anything that could be helpful. I do know she said she used to go there sometimes just to get away for a few days. It's funny that we didn't think of that before."

Harriet smiled. "I think maybe we've been concentrating too much on some possible dramatic catastrophe. We might have to settle for something more mundane."

"You may well be right, Harriet, but we have to make sure Laura's okay, especially after Eduardo's murder," replied Karen. Her patience with Harriet was running low.

"Of course," agreed Harriet.

"It's something to look into," Robert said. "Where do we begin?"

"I think we go back to the source of all human knowledge—the Internet," Ellen said. "Tomorrow, Sandra and I can look for Lamberts in the Pennsylvania land records and property deeds. That okay with you, Sandy?"

"Sure. I have a couple of appointments I can reschedule. I'm game for another day of find-it-online. I'll come to your place around nine in the morning, and we'll get started. It may be a real needle in a haystack, but I can't think of anything more useful to do right now."

"My old boss in Rome was a friend of the family. He's gone now, but I'll contact his son and see if he knows anything about the Lambert family," Robert said.

"You knew her maiden name all along, and we spent hours trying to find it online. We should have talked to you in the first place," Ellen said with a laugh.

"You gals are amazing! I'm really impressed with what you can dig up online," Robert replied, bringing big smiles to both Ellen and Sandra.

"We'll let you know what we find," Sandra said to the group as they dispersed.

The air was getting nippy when they left Riverview to cross the lawn to Oak Hall. Harriet's cottage was nearby, and Robert headed to his cottage farther up the river. The others chatted quietly as they entered the lobby and then went to their apartments. It had been a long day. The emotional turmoil they felt with Laura's disappearance had left them drained. They needed rest.

CHAPTER FOURTEEN

A Matter Is Settled.
A New Search Begins

Let my words like vegetables be tender and sweet,
for tomorrow I may have to eat them.

—ANONYMOUS

W hen Robert awoke the next morning, he rolled over and thought about the whole Laura situation. He was eager to call Sandra as soon as possible. He smiled as he assured himself, *I can call at eight thirty. Surely she'll be up then. She'll be really glad to have the new information I got last night.*

Indeed, Sandra was delighted to hear his news and assured Robert he was giving them a big head start on their search.

Unfortunately, he could not bask in the pleasure of her enthusiasm. His smile faded rapidly when his thoughts turned to Nora. After careful thought, Robert had decided that it wasn't wise to delay any longer in getting back to her. She had carried her grievances long enough and needed to know how mistaken she had been in her belief about Laura's relationship with her uncle.

Also, he still was not totally convinced she was not involved in some way in Laura's disappearance. Though she did not seem to know Laura had asked to have her reassigned, it was possible that she had found out and that they had had an argument over it. Nora did not seem to be a violent person, but she was certainly very angry at Laura, and Robert did not know what she was capable of if she became enraged. So often after a violent act, the neighbors tell the press, "He always seemed like such a nice, quiet man. Who would have thought he could do such a thing?"

Realizing he would have to be very tactful with this conversation, he decided to call Cathy, who might suggest how best to approach Nora. He knew Cathy was often in the office on weekends catching up on mail and other matters.

Robert called at 9:00 and was pleased to hear Cathy's cheerful voice. After briefly stating his case, he said, "I'd like to talk with Nora at the earliest opportunity. How soon could I do that?"

Cathy thought for a moment. "Today's Saturday, and she's on the schedule. I know that housekeepers who work on Saturdays are only here half a day. A conversation now will have the added advantage of giving her the weekend to digest the news before returning on Monday. Perhaps I could arrange for you to meet her when she finishes work."

"Sounds good. It's bound to be a shock to her to learn she's been so wrong all this time. Oh, I have another question. Do you have any suggestions as to where we could meet? We need a quiet place since it's hard to know how Nora will react."

"That room where you met with her the first time is private and will be available. Your conversation shouldn't take long, and it wouldn't be far from the café at lunchtime."

Robert welcomed the suggestion with relief. "Meetings just before lunch are seldom prolonged. I don't want to drag out my explanation of what really happened."

"It won't be easy for her to accept that she's carried such a deep resentment because of a mistaken story based on gossip instead of fact."

"As always, Cathy, you've been very helpful. Thanks."

"On the contrary, I thank *you*. I was very disturbed by Laura's refusal to have Nora in her apartment. We can never be quite sure that a personnel problem won't lead to something worse. I'll arrange for Nora to go to the card room when she finishes work. That should be at eleven-thirty."

"I'll be there." Robert let out a sigh of relief.

Just after 11:30, Nora arrived in the card room and saw Robert seated at a table. She stepped back in surprise as he stood. "Oh Mr. Symonds, I got a message from Mrs. Evans to be here after work. I wondered what it was about."

"Everything's okay, Nora. I asked her to arrange for us to meet. I'd like to give you some information, and I believe you'll think it's good news. Won't you sit?"

Nora sat slowly. Her face was a picture of anxious anticipation. Once again, she was clasping and unclasping her hands nervously as she averted her eyes.

Robert began to carefully explain that he had conducted a computer search and had learned Mrs. Lambert could not have been the woman who had beguiled her uncle. "It seems your uncle and his present wife, Sylvia, were careful to not be seen together in the office or in public. Unfortunately, some of your office colleagues made some assumptions that weren't right. I urge you to check for yourself."

Nora was taken aback. Twice she asked, "But what about …?" raising questions about matters on which her opinion had been based, and Robert explained what had actually happened. She could not disagree with his facts.

After sitting quietly for a while, still clasping and unclasping her hands, she looked up. "Well, maybe you're right, Mr. Symonds, but I really did believe it was Mrs. Lambert. After hearing your story, I'm beginning to think that my anger and resentment might have been based a lot more on what I heard than on the facts. Oh, I saw Mrs. Lambert in the office all right. We saw him with her quite a few times when she was getting her divorce. She was so attractive, at least for her age, and they both smiled and laughed a lot when they were together. Then later, I knew he was gone from the office a lot, and then there was all the chaos at home where life took a terrible turn … and trouble with Aunt Nan. We had to move out and find a new home, and I had to find a new job."

Nora stopped talking and put her head in her hands for a few seconds. Recovering, she looked up. "You know, I think you may be right, Mr. Symonds. I always accepted the office gossip that the vamp who had stolen Uncle Bud was Mrs. Lambert. After I left, my friend Gladys would call me every once in a while and pass along the office news, even after my uncle had left town. I don't have a computer, so I didn't know I could have checked for myself."

Robert was relieved to see Nora calming down after her shock and distress. He gave her a small pad with pertinent notes and urged her to go to the public library, where she could find a librarian who could help her find the records to confirm what he had told her.

Nora was thoughtful. "I wondered when I was transferred if Mrs. Lambert had asked for a new housekeeper. I don't know. Maybe it was because I was so upset two weeks ago. She wanted me to shake out a throw rug, and I thought it was a dumb idea. I guess my attitude showed, and I know some of the things I said were pretty rude. She didn't like it at all. I guess I wouldn't blame her for not wanting me around. But, please believe me, I really did think she was the reason for my troubles."

Robert was glad Nora did not break down and cry.

She said quietly, "I should thank you, Mr. Symonds. I'm so sorry about all this. Is there anything I can do to help things out?"

"Don't worry. I don't think Mrs. Lambert has any idea what you thought about her, so maybe you could simply apologize for your outburst. Let her know something had been bothering you and it must have shown, and then assure her it's all over now. If you want to, you can tell her you're sorry it upset her. Or you can do nothing and just leave it where it stands. I'm glad it's over for your sake."

As he slowly walked back to his cottage, Robert mulled over his conversation with Nora. Her reaction to his news had almost convinced him that angry as she might have been, Nora had played no role in Laura's disappearance. They would have to look elsewhere for answers.

❧

Sandra was excited when she arrived at Ellen's apartment at five to nine. "I'm glad you don't mind

I'm here early, but I just couldn't wait to tell you about Robert's call a few minutes ago. Remember? He had a boss in the early years of his career who was family friends with Laura's dad. Well, that boss died some years ago, but Robert is still good friends with his son. Anyway, last night, he called the son and got the name of Laura's father, William, and her grandfather, John—no middle names. Of course, Lambert is the last name of both. Can you believe it?"

Ellen was anxious to get started. "That'll save us lots of time! I'm glad you suggested that we enlist Robert. He's been so helpful. Let's get to work."

They went into the den, and Sandra opened her laptop.

"It's strange the Lamberts would have a place in Pennsylvania. Laura's from Boston," Ellen said.

"That's true. She's definitely from *Bah*ston," Sandra said, "but the earlier Lambert families had lived in the Philadelphia area. Laura's dad, William, went to Harvard Med and stayed up there in Massachusetts. Robert's source said that William was never called Bill or Willie or any other nickname, just Dr. William Lambert."

"How about Laura's grandfather?"

Sandra recalled what Robert had told her. "Looks like we're on the right track. The boss's son remembered him as a well-respected elderly gentleman in Philadelphia who was always called Mr. Lambert. He was sure the first name was John. The family had settled in Pennsylvania just before the Revolutionary War, and Laura's ancestor fought alongside George Washington. She's even eligible to join the DAR if she's interested. Apparently, they sold most of the land but kept the farmhouse in the family, and over the years, it was rebuilt a few times."

Ellen said with a smile, "That's great information. And I learned a little more last night—couldn't wait! I figured we should start by finding out for sure how Pennsylvania keeps track of property ownership."

"Most states do that county by county."

Ellen nodded. "And so does Pennsylvania. There's a recorder of deeds in each county, and that's where all the records are kept. I googled the names of counties near Philadelphia that could have been settled by early colonists and would still have some rural areas today with old farmhouses."

"Good for you. I was exhausted last night and went to bed before the ten o'clock news. I wanted to be on the ball this morning. I'm assuming we'll use your desktop again today."

Ellen said, "Oh yes. It's faster than your laptop."

"Did you find any place you'd recommend for a first search?"

"Yes," Ellen said. "I figure we might as well start with what I consider the most obvious place. Bucks County is northeast of Philadelphia and extends to the New Jersey border. William Penn first settled that area. As a matter of fact, I found out last night that in the early days, Pennsylvania had only three counties, and Bucks was one of them. It was much bigger then. Went all the way up north to the New York bord—"

"That was all *one* county?"

"Yep, but it's much smaller now. It's always been a popular place to live since the early days. It's scenic and so near Philly, and it's always had an artsy reputation."

Ellen smiled as her computer screen came to life. "Let's try the Bucks County website and hope to find a link to the recorder of deeds. We'll hope they're up to date with their record keeping and not still using quill pens."

Sandy grinned. "I think we'll get lots of answers online. At least we'll find out if an owner's name is enough to find out if that person owns land and where it is."

"I'm excited," Ellen exclaimed as the recorder of deeds link appeared; it offered a lot of pertinent information and instructions.

The women immersed themselves in their search and were happily surprised to find that many records were available online. The data was recorded in index books each covering five or six years.

Sandra was elated. "This perhaps means we won't have to drive two or three hours to the county seat in Doylestown and page through dusty volumes."

"Besides, it's Saturday, and the office would surely be closed anyway," Ellen said as she began to enter the information they had. They were looking for property owned by Dr. William Lambert who probably would have inherited it from John Lambert sometime in the late 1900s.

"Let's start in the 1994 to 1999 index book and work back from there," Ellen said.

The search was surprisingly quick; they went back only to the 1980 to 1988 index book. "Eureka!" exclaimed Sandra. "Here's Dr. William J. Lambert... land and house ... October 12, 1980. That has to be it! It looks like the middle initial is J. Maybe John is his middle name, like his father."

Ellen said, "Great! Let's look at the deed and see what we find. It's on page 846. I can't believe how easy this is."

The records indicated that Laura's father had inherited the property from his father. Both names were on the deed, confirming that Ellen and Sandra had been successful.

Sandra stood. She was too excited to sit. "We have to look at the property description to get the location. Is there an address?"

"The post office address is Morrisville, but it's not in town," Karen said.

They studied the deed to decipher the legalese and determined that the five-acre plot was on PA 532.

"There's a lot more blah blah blah. Let's print this out and then go on Google Maps."

"Perfect!" Sandra said. "I can't wait to share the news with the others."

CHAPTER FIFTEEN

A Busy Saturday

*Every morning when I wake up I say
I'll never be as young as I am today. Today is the
youngest day of the rest of my life. Get up and do
something fun.*

—ROCHELLE FORD,
seventy-eight-year-old sculptor

While Ellen and Sandra were working hard to find property records for Laura's family, the other women went about their usual Saturday activities. Karen spent most of the morning in the exercise room working with Bruce, Oakwood's fitness trainer. After a car accident two years earlier, Karen needed help to regain her mobility. After completing her course of physical therapy, she turned to the exercise program at Oakwood. Bruce was a tall, heavily muscled man in his late twenties who had joined the Oakwood staff three years earlier after finishing a master's in exercise physiology. He enjoyed helping older people maintain their level of fitness as long as possible, but he especially liked to work with those residents who had suffered strokes or injuries and needed to regain physical mobility.

He found that Oakwood residents were eager to work with him; they were happy and had a relaxed attitude toward exercise in marked contrast to the younger, hard-driving, perfectionists who populated many gyms and fitness centers. Those fitness jocks—male and female—were so serious and competitive that it took much of the joy out of the exercise process. The Oakwood residents were serious about maintaining their muscle tone, especially walking and balance, but they were always in good spirits and had a sense of humor about their athletic shortcomings and incipient arthritis.

Bruce had designed an exercise regimen for Karen that included workouts on the machines as well as participation in the exercise classes he conducted. That morning, there was the 9:30 exercise class and a brief workout on the NuStep machine. She had considered doing a few laps in the pool but decided she didn't feel like dealing with wet hair. She wanted to stop by the library to pick up a book listed among the new arrivals in the weekly Oakwood newsletter. She knew it would be very popular and wanted to get to it before another resident checked it out.

As Karen pumped her arms and legs on the exercise machine, she looked out the window at the view. The recreation center, between Oak Hall and the health care center, offered a view of the lawn sloping gently to the river. The cottages were along the water on the right, and the Riverview dining room was on the left. She saw several boats taking advantage of one of the few remaining days warm enough for sailing.

She spotted Henry and Martha strolling along the path next to the river. *Are they holding hands?* She couldn't be sure. Their hands were not in clear view, but they were engrossed in conversation, heads bent toward each other. *Hmmm. What's going on between them?* she asked herself a little enviously as she finished her thirty minutes on the machine. *Oh well, it's really none of my business*, she scolded herself as she carefully got off the machine and reached for her cane.

Her knee wasn't improving much, but it wasn't getting any worse, and she was hoping that with time and exercise, she would not have to rely so much on her cane. She was satisfied that she had done her best that day by going through the regimen Bruce had laid out for her. She was determined to get her old life back; she did not want to wallow in self-pity. Her body had been strong once and would be so again if she had anything to do with it. She struck her cane on the sidewalk with extra force as if for punctuation. Leaving the recreation center, she set off for the library in Oak Hall.

❧

Harriet was exercising her mind at the Oakwood library, where she was in charge of the card catalog and the circulation records. She loved the rich wood paneling that gave the room a sense of old-world elegance. It had served the original owner as a study; the built-in bookshelves and large stone fireplace made it the ideal reading room and library. Cozy chairs with nearby lamps were in niches around the room; the atmosphere was one of relaxed comfort. Harriet was always happy sitting in the room, which reminded her of her father's study with its large desk and brown leather easy chairs. He would spend Sunday afternoons at his desk planning next week's sermon since few other activities were considered appropriate for a Methodist minister on the Sabbath.

Harriet was cataloging the new books that had come in during the week. With her flair for organization, she was an ideal volunteer for the library committee. Though she was not a trained librarian, her background in social work had taught her to keep precise records, and her longtime love affair with books made her passionate about their care.

Upon arriving at Oakwood, she had carefully studied the many resident committees available: music, investment, library, bridge, garden, speaker series, sports, book club, food services, flowers, and many others. She felt it her duty to contribute to the community by working on some of the committees. After attending a few meetings of various groups, she decided she could best serve Oakwood on the library, book club, and speaker series committees. Her favorite was the library committee. She loved sitting quietly in the room surrounded by walls full of books, many of which she was eager to read or reread. She felt this was her perfect niche.

"Do you have that new book by Sarah Golin, or has it already been taken?" asked Karen as she entered the library after her exercise regimen.

"I'm just finishing it up now. I put it aside for you. You can be the first to check it out," Harriet said. She glued the cardholder on the inside of the back cover of the new book. The Oakwood library had not yet made the transition to a computer-based library system and still relied on the familiar old card catalog. However, it had recently added a text magnifying machine for residents with vision problems.

Karen happily signed the card with her name and phone extension. "I've been waiting for this to come in. From the reviews, it sounds even better than her last one."

"I've just about finished up here and was thinking of going to the cafeteria for lunch. Would you like to join me?" Harriet asked.

"Love to. I'm starving after my morning exercises. Let's go." *Maybe Harriet isn't so bad after all,* she thought.

Harriet closed the drawers of the card catalog, put away her materials, and dimmed the lights. The library was always left open for residents, so the book borrowing was done on an honor system. Fortunately, theft wasn't a serious problem. The biggest complaint was that some residents forgot to bring books back, but a short reminder note usually solved the problem.

As the two women walked down the hall to the cafeteria, Barbara came in the side door from the recreation center.

"There you are, Karen! I looked for you in the exercise room after my art class, but they said you'd left," Barbara said.

"I left early. We were just headed for the cafeteria. Want to come?" Karen asked.

"Sure. Why not?" said Barbara. "I'm not too hungry, but a soup and salad sounds good. I hadn't planned to go to class because I'm so worried about Laura, but I decided the distraction might be good, and I was right. I got a lot done this morning. I'm pleased with the way this project is going."

Responding to psychological research showing the positive effects of creative art activities on cognitive functioning, Oakwood had recently added a well-equipped art studio in the rec center designed in large part by the residents. There was plenty of storage space for paper, paints, and other art supplies in a walk-in closet. A number of easels were scattered around the room, and the center of the room was taken up by four long tables that provided space for artists to spread out their paper or canvas, paints, water containers, and other materials. Next door was a large gallery with rotating art shows of original paintings of varying quality by Oakwood residents.

Barbara had chosen to participate in the art committee since that was by far the most interesting activity for her. She was delighted with the amount of space available there; she did not want to clutter her apartment with an easel and other art equipment. She painted primarily in the art studio and confined her art activities in her apartment to sketching. She had recognized in college that she did not have the talent to succeed as a professional artist, so she had focused on art history instead. However, she had continued to enjoy creating art, and through the years, she had always set aside time for painting.

The three-hour Saturday morning classes were run by residents who took turns teaching a class in media of their choice. Barbara preferred watercolors and acrylics but could also demonstrate in oils or pastels if asked. In addition, she occasionally took a class at a nearby community center to learn some new techniques and get ideas for paintings. She was sorry that the nearest museum that offered adult art classes was a little too far to be practical especially in the winter.

The three women moved quickly through the cafeteria line. Barbara got a salad and a cup of French onion soup while the other two opted for Reuben sandwiches with chips and iced tea. They sat at a table near a sunny window.

"Harriet, I know you've been curious about the relationship between Henry and Martha," said Barbara as they took their seats.

"So am I," said Karen. "I just saw them walking along the river, and it looked like they were holding hands. Not that it's any of our business."

"I got the whole story from Sandra," Barbara said. "I knew something had happened but didn't know what it was until Sandra filled me in. It seems about a month ago, Henry found Martha in tears standing in the hallway of her apartment building. He was on the way to the barbershop for a haircut but never got there. When he found out what had happened, he immediately offered to help her."

"I thought something was going on between them," said Harriet.

"Sandra said Martha's grandson had introduced her to the computer, and she enjoyed using Skype to see and hear her newest granddaughter, who was born in Sydney. But her sense of mastery was dashed when her computer began acting up and wouldn't respond to her commands. Then a message appeared on the screen telling her that her computer had a virus and she needed to call a phone number to get help. The man who answered offered to resolve the problem but wanted two hundred and fifty dollars for the repairs. She promptly arranged payment and waited for her computer to respond."

Barbara paused to catch her breath. "She realized her mistake when she got a second message saying the computer was almost fixed but an additional four hundred dollars was now required to complete the job. In a panic, she called her bank and closed her account though of course the two hundred and fifty was already gone. Henry tried to console her by telling her that she could have lost much more if she hadn't closed the account.

"However, Martha was still upset. She was sure her computer was ruined. Henry suggested they go to her apartment and see what could be done. He knew Sandra was a computer expert and called her for help. She went to the apartment immediately and showed them that the answer was as simple as holding down the power button to close down the computer and then use System Restore after restarting it."

"No wonder Martha is so grateful to Henry and seems to hang on his every word," remarked Harriet. "I'm glad he and Sandra were able to help her. I know how important a computer can be once you start using it."

"I'm just as glad I never got addicted to one," said Karen. "I'm sure I would have all kinds of problems with it. I just don't need the hassle. Besides, I like to have face-to-face communication and to actually hold a book in my hands and make notes in the margins. No email or ebooks for me."

As they were getting up to leave, Barbara's neighbor, Eileen, stopped by their table. "Where's Laura? She wasn't at line dancing this morning. I always stand behind her so I can follow her steps if I get confused."

"Well—" Barbara began but was quickly interrupted by Harriet.

"She's away for a few days. She should be back next week in time for line dancing."

"Oh good," Eileen said. "I was afraid she was ill or had fallen or something. I'm relieved that's not it. See you later." She moved on.

"Why did you lie to her?" Barbara asked Harriet.

"I didn't lie," Harried responded stiffly. "She is away. We've established that much, and I do think she'll be back by next Saturday. I didn't want her to think we were concerned. As you know, Laura is well liked around here, and if we told her Laura was missing and we had no idea where she was, it would be all over Oakwood in twenty-four hours. Then when she returns, everyone would be asking her, 'What happened? Where were you?' You can imagine how much Laura would like that."

"I guess you're right," Barbara said with a sigh. "We don't want her to become the object of speculation. But I have to admit I'm getting more and more worried about her especially since that Italian guy's murder. It just doesn't make sense."

"It doesn't make sense because we don't have all the facts," Harriet said. "But I'm beginning to think you're right to be worried. The murder does raise new concerns about her disappearance. I really did think she would be back by now."

"I just hope Sandra and Ellen are able to find that farm or someplace where Laura might have gone," Karen said. "I keep racking my brain about what it was she'd said about a place in the country. I'm sure she mentioned it one time when she asked me to water her plants because she was going to be gone for a week or so."

"And who is the woman who called her the day she left? I think it's possible that the phone call might be related to Laura's disappearance," Harriet said. "We can talk about it over dinner tonight."

"I'll make a reservation for the group tonight. I'm also anxious to hear what Sandra and Ellen have found. Why don't you all come to my place around five for a drink before dinner? It's Saturday night after all," Karen said. She was anxious to try a new drink from her bartenders' guide, a Cozy Cosmopolitan.

"That sounds good," said Barbara.

"Yes," Harriet nodded. "Good idea. Thanks."

CHAPTER SIXTEEN
Dinner Again

It is a capital mistake to theorize before one has data. Insensibly one begins to twist facts to fit the theories, instead of theories to suit facts.

—SHERLOCK HOLMES

"This is the fourth time we've had dinner together this week," said Karen as she sat at their usual table. "I feel like I'm neglecting all my other friends."

"I can't rest easy until Laura shows up or we find out what's happened to her," replied Barbara.

The other women soon arrived followed a short time later by Robert, who was beginning to feel somewhat self-conscious about spending so much time with the Tuesday Table Ladies. Dinner at Oakwood was a social event that the residents always looked forward to, and that often provided entertainment as diners studied the room and observed who was eating with whom. Harriet was not the only resident who was interested in social patterns of the other diners, and Robert was sure his frequent dinners with the women were duly noted by other residents.

As soon as they were seated, Emily appeared with menus and water and wine glasses. She reported that the night's special was salmon teriyaki with fried rice and oriental vegetables. The other offerings—coq au vin and pork tenderloin with peach chutney—were listed on the menu along with side dishes and desserts.

After Emily took their orders and wine was poured, the group turned eagerly to Ellen and Sandra, waiting to hear what they had discovered. Everyone had chosen the caprese salad on the menu; no one wanted to miss anything by going to the salad bar.

"Did you find out anything?" asked Barbara.

"A lot," Sandra said. "But we couldn't have done it without Robert's help."

All eyes turned to him.

"I'm glad it helped," he said. "I have some other news too, but I'll wait until you two tell us what you found in the land records."

Ellen quickly explained how Robert had given them the names of Laura's father and grandfather and how they had tracked down the property deed to a parcel of land in Bucks County, Pennsylvania. "We were very lucky and hit pay dirt right away in that county. The property is near Morrisville, about a hundred and twenty miles north of here."

"Morrisville," mused Karen. "Now that you say it, I do seem to remember Laura mentioning that name once when she asked me to take in a package she was expecting. I didn't pay much attention because she was going to be gone only a few days." Karen was always glad to realize her memory was not failing her.

"Here's where the farm is," said Sandra, passing around the Google map they had printed out. The property was clearly marked. "It's about a two-and-a-half-hour drive from Oakwood."

"Now what do we do?" asked Harriet, who had been uncharacteristically quiet up to then.

"Let's hear what else Robert has found out." Barbara suggested, turning to Robert expectantly.

At that moment, Emily arrived with their salads. He waited until everyone had been served. "Just before leaving the house, I received a call from my friend Steve. That's why I was a little late."

"I thought he was back in Rome," Sandra said. "Has he already returned to the States?"

"No, he's still there and he has gotten some pretty interesting information about Eduardo." He had their full attention.

"What did he find out?" Barbara asked impatiently.

"Steve was asked by the authorities to inform Eduardo's next of kin of his death and see what they wished to do with his body. His mother is in her late nineties and pretty frail, but his older brother and his family live with her in their village outside Rome. They asked to have the body cremated and the ashes returned to Italy for burial in the family cemetery." Robert paused while Emily served the entrees and removed the salad dishes.

"Steve took the opportunity to question the brother further about the smuggling ring and asked whether he knew anything about it. It seems that back then, Eduardo had indeed been asked by art thieves to smuggle art objects across Europe in his race car and had turned them down. He was very indignant that anyone would think he would agree to do something illegal. He had talked it over with his brother, and they thought it might be too dangerous to go to the police with the information.

It was common knowledge that the local police department was infiltrated with spies for various gangs, so they decided to keep quiet. Of course, that was over forty years ago, during Eduardo's prime racing days."

"Wow," said Ellen. "This sounds like a crime novel."

"What about the icon?" asked Barbara. "Did he say anything about that?"

"Yes," Robert replied. "It's an interesting story. Our hunch that it might have been a gift to Laura from Eduardo was correct, and as we suspected, he was hoping to persuade her to return it to him. It seems that Laura's icon is an old Giotti family heirloom that had been passed down to the oldest son on his wedding day for over three hundred years. When Eduardo, the second son, impulsively gave it to Laura, the family was furious, and even more so when they learned she had taken it with her back to Boston."

"He must have been really serious about her to give her such a family treasure," remarked Sandra thoughtfully.

"Or else he was just really immature and impulsive," Harriet commented acerbically.

"But that was years and years ago," Ellen pointed out. "Why now? Why was he after her to give it up now?"

"Apparently, the older brother, who should have received the icon in the first place, has a grandson who is to be married soon, and as the oldest son of the oldest son, the icon should rightfully have gone to him on his wedding day. Eduardo was very close to this great-nephew and felt so bad about having given the icon away. He wanted to make it up to the family by bringing the icon back to Italy in time for the wedding. That's why he seemed so desperate to speak to Laura. He came to the States to meet her face to face to persuade her to return it. The Giottis have cousins in New Jersey who were able to get her address and phone number so he could contact her."

Everyone had stopped eating. The women looked at each other in shocked surprise.

"And he was killed before he could meet her," said Karen thoughtfully.

"Or perhaps while he was meeting with her," Sandra added.

"Even if she was there and they argued about the icon, I can't believe Laura would have killed him," Harriet said.

"No, she couldn't do such a thing," Barbara insisted. "Besides, she's not strong enough to kill him. Surely he would have fought back. But it's possible that she might have been with him when he was killed and that she was also attacked by the murderer. If she witnessed the murder, she might have been kidnapped. There are so many terrible things that might have happened to her," Barbara said, near tears.

"Oh my gosh," Ellen said. "This is absolutely surreal."

The others sat silently, looking uneasily at each other as Emily approached to remove the dinner plates. As she removed the plates, Emily asked cheerily, "Are you all ready for dessert?"

"I'll just have coffee with cream," Harriet replied soberly. The others ordered coffee or tea. No one felt like eating dessert.

Karen turned to Robert. "Now what? Do you think Eduardo had a chance to talk to Laura in person before he was killed?"

"I don't know. It's possible," said Robert. "As someone suggested, she might have been with him when he was attacked and was injured herself or was frightened and has gone into hiding. On the other hand, her disappearance might be unrelated to his death, but we won't know for sure until we find her. Neither the newspaper nor Steve mentioned anything about a woman being seen with him."

"But if the icon wasn't stolen and the art thieves weren't after that, could they still have killed him for some reason?" asked Barbara. "Or was it just a random violent act?"

"I'm afraid we don't have an answer to that," replied Robert. "His money wasn't taken, so robbery wasn't the motive. That was one reason the authorities thought it was related to the Italian gang, and it's still possible they're involved. I hope to hear from Steve when the police get more evidence."

"Do you all think that perhaps the woman who called here looking for Laura was calling on behalf of Eduardo?" Barbara asked.

"At this point, anything's possible," Sandra said. "She could even have been calling for the killers who were trying to find Eduardo."

"It's possible that the phone call is related to Eduardo's murder," said Robert. "Or it might be tied in with Laura's disappearance in another way. We know Laura was apparently going to meet someone somewhere. At the moment, the best bet for where is this farmhouse in Bucks County you two located. In addition to Eduardo, the best bet for whom she might have gone to meet could be the mysterious caller who spoke to her the day she disappeared."

"We know Laura's car is missing, so presumably, she drove herself wherever she went. She may have picked someone up or met them someplace," Barbara said.

"Or perhaps she just wanted to get away by herself for a while," suggested Harriet, who sometimes felt that way herself.

"But we know she had her hair done. Patty got the impression she was meeting someone," replied Barbara.

"Sitting around talking about it isn't getting us anywhere," Karen said. "The only lead we have now is the house in Bucks County. Is there a phone listed for that residence?" she asked, nervously rubbing her cane.

"No. We checked on that as soon as we got the address," replied Sandra. "They must rely on cell phones, and we know Laura's has been turned off."

"And it's still turned off," added Ellen. "We tried it again."

"I think the only logical option is to drive up there and check it out," said Barbara. "It's only a couple of hours from here, and tomorrow is Sunday. I think we should go."

"But not all of us," said Sandra. "We can't all go barging in on her if she's there. What if she has a man there for a romantic weekend?"

"Oh my God. That never occurred to me," said Ellen. "Do you really think that's a possibility? Maybe Harriet's right and we are a bunch of old busybodies prying into her personal life."

"I think with Eduardo's murder occurring right when he was trying to meet with Laura, we do have some reason for concern," Harriet said, surprising the others. "I think we need to check it out now that we have an address. The question is who should go."

"I want to go," said Barbara firmly. "I have to be doing something. I feel responsible for bringing her into the Tuesday group. I couldn't possibly sit around here waiting to hear from you all."

"I'll go with you," said Karen. "I feel some responsibility too because she's my neighbor. Does anyone else want to go?"

The other women shook their heads, but Robert spoke up. "I'll be glad to drive you. I don't know that there's any real danger, but we aren't sure of what you might find. I think it would be a good idea to have a man along."

The two women sighed in relief. They had to admit that it would be reassuring to have Robert with them.

"Do we get to ride in your Jaguar?" asked Barbara.

"Sure. It's the only car I have," replied Robert with a smile.

"Now the rest of us are going to be jealous," Sandra said with a laugh.

"We'll leave the first thing in the morning and should be back before dinner," Robert said. "I guess you had better make dinner reservations again for tomorrow night. Hopefully, we'll have good news to report."

"Why don't you pick us up at the front entrance of our building at nine? There won't be much traffic on the roads on Sunday morning, so we should make good time," Karen said, relieved they were actually going to do something.

Robert picked up the map Sandra and Ellen had passed around. "This will be a big help, and I have my phone's GPS as a backup. My old Jag doesn't have such modern devices. I'll fill Cathy in on what we're up to," Robert said. "She's worried about Laura as well as any possible adverse publicity for Oakwood, so I want to keep her in the loop. I'll see you two in the morning." He rose.

Harriet said, "Good night" and headed to her cottage while the others strolled to their apartments, mulling over the disturbing news they had received. They wondered what the next day would bring.

CHAPTER SEVENTEEN
Laura's Story

Life shrinks or expands in proportion
to one's courage.

—ANAÏS NIN

The two women were standing under the portico at the entrance of their building when Robert pulled up in his racing green Jaguar the next morning. They shivered as Robert helped them into the car. Barbara took the front seat while Karen, armed with her cane, got in the back.

"It's really chilly this morning. I didn't realize the temperature had dropped so much since yesterday," Barbara said. "I'm glad you have the car warmed up for us. I hope the roads are okay."

"This car is amazing," exclaimed Karen, looking around the backseat. "How old is it? And where did you get it?"

"It's a 1955 Mark I 2.4-liter Jaguar," replied Robert proudly. "I inherited it from my mother. I was a teenager when she bought it and thought it was the hottest thing I'd ever seen. I had it totally rebuilt a few years ago after she died, and I'm still in love with it."

He started the car and pulled out of the Oakwood driveway.

"What did your parents do?" Barbara asked. "This must have been a pretty unusual car even in 1955."

"My dad was a banker and my mother was an actress. You may have heard of her. She was pretty well known at the time. Her stage name was Simone Dupree."

"Wow!" Barbara exclaimed. "Of course we've heard of her. She was one of the most famous actresses of her time. I can't imagine what it must have been like to have her as a mother. You must have had a very glamorous childhood."

"I spent much of it in boarding schools, but I did get to travel a lot. I've been to most of Europe, Canada, South Africa, Australia, even Singapore. All that travel probably led to my interest in the State Department, and it was certainly a good background for my career."

"We traveled a lot too, but life in a military family was very different," Karen said.

Further questioning by Barbara led Robert to tell a series of amusing anecdotes about his mother and her flamboyant escapades some of which had made headlines in entertainment weeklies at the time.

"I seem to remember a Spanish prince and your mother," Barbara said.

"Oh yes. That made all the gossip columns. My parents didn't spend a lot of time together, but they never divorced, and my mother took care of my father during his final illness. I think they were really devoted to each other despite her antics and the differences in their lifestyles."

The three lapsed into silence as their thoughts turned to what might lie before them. Barbara was thinking of the trouble Laura might be in and whether they would really find her at the farmhouse or if the trip would end up a wild goose chase. She had expected to lead an orderly, predictable life at Oakwood, giving her children peace of mind concerning her safety and well-being. But she was headed into the unknown for the sake of her old friend Laura. She could hardly believe it.

On the other hand, Karen was weighing the danger they might be heading into. At least one person was dead; surely the killer or killers wouldn't hesitate to kill again. *If we find Laura at the farmhouse, will she be alive?* She was beginning to wonder how they had gotten into this and whether it was smart of them to go to the farmhouse alone. Perhaps they should have called the police after all.

"Come to think of it, Robert, do you have a gun in the car? We really don't know what we're getting into," Karen said. "I'm a pretty good marksman. I used to win ribbons in the shooting competitions at my dad's gun club. My cane is useful in warding off would-be purse snatchers, but a gun would be more reassuring now."

"No," Robert replied. "I was trained to use firearms if necessary. Some of my overseas postings were in remote settings where we couldn't always depend on the security provided by the Marines. But I had no interest in pursuing it as a hobby. I keep my gun in a locked case in my bedroom closet." He was beginning to have second thoughts about taking the two women to this remote farmhouse. *Perhaps this isn't such a good idea.*

The two-and-a-half-hour drive seemed to take an eternity though there was little traffic on the interstate or the two-lane county road they turned onto. The heavily wooded scenery lining the highway gradually gave way to rolling hills covered with brown fields left from the fall harvest. After trying to make chitchat about the weather and activities at Oakwood, they continued the journey in uneasy silence. They had much to think about.

Robert slowed down and asked Barbara, "Can you read the name on that mailbox? I think this should be it."

"No, I can't make it out. Too faded." She was becoming more anxious as they got closer to their destination. *What if this really is a wild goose chase? What if Laura isn't here? What if it isn't even safe? This is our last lead. There are no other trails to follow.*

"I think we'll try it," Robert said, making the turn. They drove down a winding gravel driveway into dense woods with thick underbrush on both sides. They had gone only a short way when they heard what sounded like gunshots in the woods ahead of them. Robert brought the car to an abrupt halt.

"That's got to be gunfire!" exclaimed Karen.

"It sure sounded like it," Barbara said. "What on earth should we do now?"

"We can't stop," Robert said. "Let's go a little farther and hope it was just a hunter."

Robert inched the car forward. At the next turn, they saw that the driveway led up to an old, two-story stone farmhouse in a grassy yard surrounded by firs. He pulled over and stopped. Standing in front of the house was an old man wearing a battered felt hat and holding a rifle. He stood for a few seconds looking at them suspiciously, turned, and disappeared into the woods behind the house.

"He gave me quite a fright," exclaimed Karen. "I hope he's cleared off for good. You okay, Barbara?"

"Oh my," she replied. "It looks like the house in the photo, and look! There's Laura's car!"

Robert turned off the motor. "There's a second car with Pennsylvania plates. I wonder whose that might be. I think I had better go up to the house and check it out. You two wait here." He undid his seatbelt and opened the door. "Lock it."

The two women watched anxiously as Robert walked the thirty yards to the house. After looking cautiously around, he slowly climbed the front steps. Barbara unlocked the car and threw open the door. "I can't sit here any longer. You wait here in case there's trouble," she said as she stepped out.

Karen had already started to open the rear door. Ignoring Barbara's words, she determinedly climbed out of the car. Clutching her cane, she followed Barbara down the driveway toward the house.

Barbara quickly joined Robert on the porch as he reached for the old brass door knocker and rapped loudly several times. They waited anxiously on the doorstep until the door was finally opened by a very striking blond woman who looked to be in her early twenties. Karen steadily made her way up the steps to join the other two.

"Oh my! Who are you?" blurted Barbara in surprise. It was a scenario she had not anticipated.

"Who are *you?*" the young woman retorted, staring at the unexpected visitors on the doorstep.

"We apologize for disturbing you, but we're looking for Laura Lambert and wondered whether she could be here," Robert said quietly.

"Laura, can you come to the door? Some people are asking for you," the young woman called over her shoulder.

"Who in the world?" they heard Laura say as she made her way to the door. She stood motionless, staring at them in complete amazement but looking no worse for wear.

"Thank goodness you're alive!" cried Barbara in relief, stepping forward to hug her.

Laura stepped back. "Why wouldn't I be? What are you doing here?"

"We've been so worried about you," Barbara answered, dropping her arms.

"It's a long story Laura," replied Robert. "Could we come in and talk? It's pretty cold out here."

Laura looked at Karen and Barbara, who were shivering in their lightweight jackets, and stepped back wordlessly, holding the door open for them. "Of course. It's warm inside. I'm just so surprised to see you here. I'm not thinking. Do come in."

They entered a large room dominated by a massive fireplace containing a cheerful fire that was sending out waves of warm air. The two women walked to the fireplace and stretched out their hands toward the fire.

A long planked table with several chairs around it stood at one end of the room, the remains of an earlier breakfast scattered across its surface. A woman who appeared to be in her mid-to-late fifties was seated at the table with a coffee cup in her hand. She quickly rose and stepped toward the newcomers. An elderly man in a wheelchair slowly entered from a hallway at the other end of the living room near a large wooden staircase.

"What's going on out here? Oh! I didn't know we had visitors." He wheeled himself to an old leather easy chair next to the fireplace. "Won't you introduce us to the newcomers, Laura?" he asked as he carefully transferred himself to the leather chair.

Laura, still somewhat stunned, said quietly, "Dad, I'd like you to meet Karen and Barbara, friends of mine, who have arrived unexpectedly from Oakwood. Barbara and I used to work together in the law firm when I was starting out."

They all murmured greetings. Her father turned to Robert. "And who is this?"

"I think this is someone you heard about a long time ago, and he also happens to live at Oakwood. Dad, meet Robert Symonds, the young man at the American embassy in Rome who put me on the plane to Boston."

William Lambert immediately showed his pleasure with a large smile and an outstretched hand. "How amazing! I never thought I'd have the chance to thank you in person for what you did that day. Old John Herbert certainly knew what he was doing when he turned the job over to you. I still don't know how you managed it. You must tell me about it."

"Well, sir, I didn't have much choice. And it really wasn't as hard as I expected. I think perhaps they had already begun to have some second thoughts, and I gave them an excuse to change their minds. I just pointed out the reality of their future together with perhaps a little exaggeration," he said, smiling at Laura, who still seemed to be recovering from the shock of their appearance at her door.

The two men shook hands and smiled. Robert turned to the middle-aged woman who was standing with the young woman who had answered the door. Instinctively sizing up the situation, Robert asked with a smile, "Won't you introduce us to your daughter and granddaughter, Laura?" He held out his hand to the older woman. "You must be Melissa."

Laura stared at him, momentarily speechless, and then burst out, "How in the world did you know this is my daughter?"

Robert laughed. "I didn't know for sure, but the family resemblance is truly amazing. Melissa has your eyes and mouth, and your granddaughter looks exactly like that eighteen-year-old girl I met in the embassy in Rome. Don't you agree, Dr. Lambert?"

"Yes indeed. She really took my breath away when I first saw her. She's the very image of Laura at that age. I still can't get over the resemblance. I only wish Laura's mother were here to see it."

"Hi. My name is Carol." The young woman shook hands with Robert and turned to Barbara and Karen.

Karen, leaning heavily on her cane, spoke. "I think I need to sit down. I'm very confused."

Carol quickly brought chairs for Barbara and Karen and placed them near the fireplace while the other three women took seats on the sofa. Robert pulled over a straight chair and joined them.

"We weren't sure we were at the right house until we saw your car," Barbara said. "And then there was the old man with the rifle who made us even more nervous."

"That's just old Cal. He lives on the next farm and likes to go squirrel hunting in our woods. He's perfectly harmless. But I still don't understand what you all are doing here or how you found me," Laura said plaintively.

"You didn't show up for dinner Tuesday night and hadn't told us you wouldn't be there," Barbara said.

"You came looking for me because I didn't show up for dinner?" Laura was astonished.

"That's what started it," said Karen. "We were really worried because you hadn't signed out, and we couldn't reach you on your cell. Then there was the strange message from Eduardo on your answering machine."

Laura turned accusingly to Robert. "How do they know about Eduardo? What did you tell them?"

"Only that he was an old friend you had known in Rome. When they couldn't find you Tuesday night, they went to your apartment to make sure you hadn't fallen or passed out," Robert explained quietly. "They listened to a phone message he left on your machine, and he sounded so anxious to get hold of you that they were afraid you were in some kind of trouble. They didn't want to go to the police, so they were trying to find you on their own. They asked me to help them because they weren't sure what to do, and Eduardo had mentioned my name in his message."

"Does everyone at Oakwood think I'm missing?" Laura was clearly upset.

"Oh no. The Tuesday Table Ladies have been very discreet. These two were really worried about you because you're always so careful to let them know if your plans have changed," Robert said. "That's why they felt it necessary to look in your apartment," he said soothingly. Years with the State Department had prepared him to deal with emotional situations like this, and Laura soon calmed down.

"I realized later that I'd forgotten to let you know I wouldn't be at dinner and that I hadn't signed out, but I didn't think anyone would even notice or care I wasn't there. I'm really touched that you all went to so much trouble to make sure I was okay."

"Unfortunately, Laura, there's more to this. Something terrible has happened that caused us to fear you might really be in danger," Robert said gently. "I'm afraid that we are the bearers of some sad news. It involves Eduardo. He was attacked and seriously hurt on Tuesday. When we found out he was in intensive care, knowing that he'd been trying to locate you and that you were missing, we feared that you might also have been a victim of his attackers."

"Oh no! That's awful. Where is he now? How did you find out? Is he alright?"

The look on Robert's face gave her the answer. "I'm very sorry to bring you this news, but I have to tell you that Eduardo didn't make it. His injuries were too severe."

Laura and Melissa gasped simultaneously. Laura put her arms around her daughter, who started crying. "I was so hoping to meet him," stammered Melissa.

"It's my fault. I should have returned his phone calls and told him to meet us here. I just wanted a little time alone with Melissa before I had to share her with her father," Laura said almost in a whisper.

Karen and Barbara were speechless as they watched the tableau before them and wondered what was going on.

"I don't think it could have been avoided," Robert said softly. "He was attacked Tuesday afternoon, probably shortly after leaving the message on your machine. If he had come here, they might have followed him, and you'd all have been in danger. Barbara and Karen, we'll explain this in a minute. But first Laura, tell us how you and Melissa managed to find each other after all these years," said Robert smoothly, carefully changing the subject to a happier one. "Did you know you were pregnant when you left Rome?"

Barbara and Karen exchanged questioning glances.

Laura said, "No, of course not or I wouldn't have gone. Daddy wanted me to have an annulment immediately, but as soon as I realized I might be pregnant, I refused. I didn't want my baby to be illegitimate."

"That was a serious concern in those days," Dr. Lambert remarked. "She and the baby both could have been stigmatized and her life ruined. Fortunately, it's much easier for young women to keep their babies now. I dropped the annulment idea and arranged for her to stay with friends out west with an old colleague from medical school and his wife. Her mother flew out to be with her before the birth and was with her for a while afterward. She had the baby there, and no one in Boston knew anything about it. Laura was back in Boston to start college the next September. It was really hard for her to give up the baby, but in the long run, it was best for everyone." He looked at Melissa.

"After Melissa was born, I got to see her only briefly before they took her away," Laura said, looking at her daughter. "As soon as I was able to travel, Mother and I went to Reno, and I got a divorce from Eduardo."

"I insisted she let Eduardo know about the baby and the divorce, but there was no way he could get custody of the child once the adoption was complete," Dr. Lambert added.

"So Eduardo was your husband?" Barbara asked. "And you knew about it, Robert? Why on earth didn't you tell us?"

"Because it was Laura's story to tell. I told you only what was necessary, that he had known her and that he might have given her the icon he was talking about in the hospital."

"Would you please start at the beginning and tell me what brought you here?" asked Laura, still puzzled by their sudden appearance.

"First, let's offer our guests some coffee or tea," Dr. Lambert said. "Carol, would you please take care of it? I'd like a cup of tea myself."

Carol and Melissa quickly set about getting mugs of hot coffee for Robert and Karen and tea for Barbara and Dr. Lambert. They settled down to listen as the three visitors explained how the Tuesday Table Ladies, with Robert's help, had managed to trace Laura to the stone farmhouse. They left out Nora's story, but they filled in the details of the art smugglers and their possible role in Eduardo's murder.

"I'm impressed," said Dr. Lambert, smiling at the amateur detectives. "It's amazing that you were able to put the pieces together so quickly."

"We felt that time was running out when we heard of Eduardo's murder because so many terrible things could have happened to Laura," Barbara replied. "And it was Robert and his friend Steve who put together the story of Eduardo's ties to the art thieves, which we now see had nothing to do with Laura, thank goodness."

"But why was he so anxious to get the icon back?" Laura asked.

"We found that out from Steve, who had spoken with Eduardo's older brother," said Robert. He spelled out the history of the icon and its importance to the Giotti family.

"I had no idea," said Laura. "Eduardo gave it to me on our wedding day. It meant so much to me because it was my only link to those few weeks in Rome and our whirlwind romance. It was a magical time for me despite everything."

"Of course, but now you have two living links to that part of your life, and that's certainly more satisfying than a wooden artifact," Robert gently said, nodding at Melissa and Carol. "But you haven't told us how you finally managed to find each other after all this time."

"We'd both made sporadic attempts over the years, but the adoption records in the state where

Melissa was born weren't publicly available until a few months ago," Laura replied.

"I was a little hesitant to look too hard while my adoptive parents were alive," said Melissa. "They were wonderful parents, but they were always a little sensitive about adoptees searching for their birth parents. After they died a few months ago, I felt free to search more seriously, and it was around that time the state began to open up adoption records for birth parents and their children.

"When I submitted the forms, I found that Laura had already signed a document giving permission to release the original birth certificate if I requested it. That was a real breakthrough. Once we had the certificate listing my parents as Laura Lambert Giotti and Eduardo Giotti, it took almost no time for Carol to locate her on the Internet. We made the first contact shortly after I sent the note you found in her apartment. After we talked on the phone a few times, Carol and I planned to fly east to meet Laura and her father."

"When she told us Eduardo was in the country, we thought it was the perfect time to meet him, and so we moved up our visit," Carol added.

"I called Laura from the airport when we were able to get a last-minute flight to Philadelphia. I had a few minutes of panic when I couldn't get through on the cell number she'd been using, so I called the desk at Oakwood," Melissa explained. "They put me through on her land line, and we made arrangements to meet at the Philly airport that evening. I think we were all a little nervous, but of course, we spotted each other right away. As you noticed, the family resemblance is startling."

"I was so excited when I got the call from Melissa that they were on their way that I forgot about dinner and signing out and everything else. I just wanted to get to the airport in time to meet their plane. As it was, I barely made it, but I was standing there when they came through security, and thanks to the family resemblance, I recognized them immediately." Laura smiled at her daughter. "I had turned off my cell because I didn't want to talk to Eduardo until I had a little time with Melissa and Carol. Now I'm really sorry I did," she said, once again on the edge of tears.

Carol put her arms around her grandmother. "I feel so lucky that we've found you and Grandpa Lambert. It would have been so wonderful to meet Eduardo as well, but I'm just glad we have you now."

"She's right," said Melissa. "Finding you has been such an incredible gift that we must not dwell on the fact that we didn't get to know Eduardo too."

"Speaking for the three of us, we're just relieved to find you alive and well," Robert said to Laura. "I'm sorry we were the bearers of such sad news, but I'm glad you heard about it while you were here with your family to support you."

"How about some lunch?" asked Dr. Lambert, changing the mood of the room. Carol and Melissa began clearing the breakfast dishes from the table and then brought out chicken salad and cold cuts for sandwiches as well as drinks. As they sat around the table enjoying the impromptu lunch, Dr. Lambert told them about the history of the farm and his family's experiences as early settlers of Bucks County. He had already given copies of the Lambert family genealogy to Melissa and Carol, but they were eager to hear more about their newfound family and hear Dr. Lambert's stories.

Barbara and Karen gave Laura more details about their activities while she was gone. "Sandra remembered that she had seen Eduardo in a race in Monte Carlo years ago. She was quite smitten even at a distance. She'll be so jealous you were actually married to him. He must have been quite hand-some," Barbara said.

"He was," replied Laura. "And it was such a glam-orous environment, a constant circus. Whenever we went out, we were quickly surrounded by paparazzi who were always taking pictures. In fact, I have an old newspaper article I brought along to show Melissa and Carol. I'll get it."

She quickly returned with a yellowed clipping enclosed in a protective plastic sleeve and handed it to Barbara. The text was in Italian, but the photo showed a beautiful blond girl with a very handsome, dark-haired young man. They were laughing as they looked directly into the camera.

"I can see what Robert meant," said Karen. "This picture of you could easily be mistaken for one of Carol. You two are identical twins separated by time."

"Eduardo is absolutely gorgeous," Barbara exclaimed. "No wonder you fell for him so quickly."

"He was really very sweet," Laura said softly, obviously moved by the memory of the handsome young man.

"You made a beautiful couple. You really seem to go together somehow," Barbara said as she studied the clipping.

"That's how we felt," responded Laura, looking again at the photo. "But Robert and Dad were right. It would never have worked out in the long run. We were just too different, and we really wanted different things. Or thought we did." Laura returned the photo to the other room, and the women finished their lunch.

Robert and Dr. Lambert had been discussing their mutual friend, Robert's old boss, whose son had given him the last bit of information needed to locate Laura. "He said to tell you hello. He has fond memories of you from years ago when your two families used to vacation together," Robert reported.

They rose from the table. Robert said, "I think it's time to be heading back to Oakwood. The rest of the Tuesday Table Ladies are waiting to hear whether we've found you and if you're all right. I can't get through on my cell phone, and I want to reassure them that you are here with your family and that you are more than okay."

"Yes, our cell phone service comes and goes," said Laura. "Thank you so much for going to all this trouble." She hugged each of them at the door. "I'm truly overwhelmed that you all went to so much trouble to make sure I was okay. I'm really lucky to have found such good friends at Oakwood. And please thank the others for me too. It'll be great to see everyone there. I'm going to bring Melissa and Carol back with me to show them where I live and let them meet the rest of the Tuesday Table Ladies. I wasn't sure how I was going to explain the sudden appearance of these two," she said, smiling. "It's a complicated story."

"We'll fill in Harriet, Ellen, and Sandra," said Karen. "You can just tell anyone else that they're your daughter and granddaughter visiting from out west. They don't need to know any more than that."

As the three climbed into Robert's car, Carol yelled, "Hey, that's some cool car. Can I get a ride in it when we come to Oakwood?"

"You sure can," Robert replied. "I might even let you drive!"

CHAPTER EIGHTEEN
The Reunion

*You don't choose your family. They are God's gift
to you, as you are to them.*

—DESMOND TUTU

It was Tuesday night. Harriet stood to greet Barbara and Sandra as they came to the table. "I see the hostess directed you to this bigger table. We have nine people tonight instead of the usual six members of the Tuesday Table group."

Sandra was excited. "I can hardly wait to see Laura again. I haven't gotten a thing done since Sunday night when we heard about the happenings up in Bucks County."

"I think all of us are running in high gear," Barbara said. "I just can't imagine how overwhelmed Laura must be about her daughter and granddaughter, though I must say that she seemed calmer than any of us on Sunday."

Robert came to the table, closely followed by Ellen and Karen. He pointed to the three empty chairs. "Laura and the girls aren't here yet? I was afraid they wouldn't get away from the house as early as they planned. They probably weren't happy about leaving Dr. Lambert after their wonderful reunion."

"I'm sure that's true," Barbara said, "but it's really better for him to stay there where he's comfortable and well taken care of. Laura said his caregiver is really sweet. She seems almost like a member of the family. We didn't meet her because they'd given her the day off on Sunday."

"Yes," added Karen, "and they will probably be going back up before too long for another visit."

As soon as everyone was seated, Kevin came to the table to say he would be their server that night because Emily had a big exam coming up. "I notice you have extra chairs. Would you like to wait for the others to arrive? I can take your drink orders now."

"We'll wait a bit for dinner orders," Harriet said, "but we'll have some ice water all around, no lemon for the two ladies at the end of the table. We'll need wine glasses too. You'd better bring seven." She scanned the others at the table. "Anything else?"

Karen requested iced tea, and Ellen ordered cranberry juice. Kevin jotted down the orders, distributed menus, and left.

Harriet settled back in her chair but straightened right up as she saw Henry Gresham and Martha Foster being seated at a table for two by a window. "Seems Henry and Martha are eating together again tonight. That's getting to be a habit with them."

"This morning, I saw them ambling along on the walking trail together again," Karen said. "I couldn't swear to it, but I think they were holding hands. I hope they were. We could use a little romance around here."

"I agree, Karen," Sandra said, "and you might be right about the holding hands. I'm pretty sure they're planning a Caribbean cruise together this fall, including the Panama Canal. Martha's mailbox is close to mine, and she and Henry often sit down on nearby chairs to look at mail together. The last couple of weeks, they've been excited about looking at cruise brochures. I think they've booked something for this fall from Ft. Lauderdale."

Further speculation about romance was interrupted by the arrival of the newly united Lambert family. Robert stepped aside to enjoy watching the greetings, introductions, hugs, laughter, and even a few tears. When Howard at the next table asked what was going on, Robert replied, "Laura's been away for a few days and has brought some of her family back for a little visit."

"The ladies do like to carry on, don't they!" Howard said lightly.

Robert smiled to himself as he helped seat the new arrivals.

The table was quiet while everyone looked at the menu. Kevin came to let them know that the catch of the day was pan-fried trout with capers. He took careful notes about everyone's order and seemed to have been particularly attentive to Carol. When he left to get the soups and salads, conversation and laughter picked up immediately and continued throughout the dinner.

Almost an hour later, after dessert was finished and coffee and tea had been refilled a couple of times, Ellen looked around the dining room. "We certainly seem to be closing the place down tonight. Only one other table is left down at the other end."

"I told Kevin a few minutes ago that we'd be hanging around for a while," Harriet said. "He'll clear the table except for our water and wine so we won't hold up the kitchen staff. This seems like a good place to talk."

As if on cue, Kevin appeared and began to clear the dessert dishes. As he got to Carol, he said, "I hope you folks enjoyed your dinner tonight."

"Yes, we did," Carol said. "There were so many good things on the menu that it was hard to choose. I loved the pork tenderloin and the fresh vegetables too."

Kevin grinned. "I'm glad. I'll tell the chefs."

Sandra couldn't resist the urge to tease Kevin a bit. She smiled. "The rest of us enjoyed our meals, too, Kevin, but we can understand why you would like to check with one of the guests in particular."

Kevin blushed. "Oh Mrs. Brown, I'm glad you enjoyed your dinner too." He picked up the last two cups and turned quickly. Carol smiled.

"Don't worry, Kevin," Sandra said with a wink. "We won't tell Emily."

Harriet sat forward. "Robert, you told me you had some new information to share with us. Now that things are quiet and more private, would this be a good time?"

Robert welcomed the opportunity. "I know we're all concerned about the circumstances of Eduardo's death, and the latest news from Steve is sad but reassuring. Laura, the women know that almost all my recent information about Eduardo has been coming from Steve, my friend and former colleague who's with the FBI. They know about your icon and that years ago there were suspicions in Europe that Eduardo had been involved with a group that was transporting stolen art."

All attention was focused on Robert as the women uncomfortably avoided eye contact with anyone else at the table.

Barbara spoke up quickly. "But we know he was never involved in that."

Heads nodded.

"That's true," Robert said. "But my latest news from Steve, who's still in Italy, is that Eduardo was definitely targeted. A breakthrough was made recently in that decades-old case. A police informant reported that the art thieves knew the authorities were beginning to close in on them. They thought that Eduardo, who had refused to go along with them, had become an informant and was going to tell the police what he knew.

"He could identify the guys who had been involved in the smuggling operation. So when Eduardo left, they assumed he was going to turn them in to the Americans. They realized Eduardo would have known he couldn't report them secretly in Italy because the smugglers had spies in the

Italian police. Therefore, they asked their contacts in America to 'take care of him,' and it looks like they did. The FBI has identified the killers, and the DC police are looking for them now. They should have them in custody before long."

During the next few minutes, those at the table shared condolences and shed tears.

"This just seems unreal, like a bad movie," Ellen murmured.

Sandra contributed an optimistic note. "Laura, at least you're okay and didn't have to witness the tragedy."

"And we're so happy to welcome two new members of the Lambert family," Karen added.

Laura leaned in. "I want all of you to know I'm very touched by your concern for me. I would never have thought I had such good friends. You know I've always been quiet about my personal life, but now, I'm happy to share the good news with you."

She took a deep breath. "You've met my daughter and granddaughter here, but you haven't heard much about how we finally got together. Actually, we're still catching up on everything ourselves, but it's a wonderful journey that we're on. My father sends his best to you. He looks forward to coming here and thanking all of you in person for your interest and your efforts. By the way, he compliments you two, Ellen and Sandra, on your computer skills.

"I'm hoping to convince him to move out of that old house and settle here. I'd worry less about him if he were nearby and close to good medical facilities. The old farmhouse is wonderful for weekends, but it's a little too remote for someone in his nineties."

Smiles and murmurs of assent were plentiful at the table.

Barbara said, "You know we told them Sunday night about everything we had learned that day, about you and Eduardo."

Laura took Melissa's hand and interrupted, "And about the adoption. That was the saddest day of my life!"

"Yes, we told them about the adoption and the divorce," Barbara said. "They also know about Melissa's happy life with her adoptive parents as well as about Carol and how they found you."

Laura smiled weakly. "So I guess we'd better fill you in and bring you up to date. After I informed Eduardo about Melissa's birth and adoption and about the divorce, of course I felt sure the Italian adventure part of my life was over. The only deep regret I always carried with me was losing Melissa, but I felt sure she was having a better life than I could have provided for her then."

Melissa squeezed her mother's hand. "And you know I'll forever be grateful to you for being so unselfish."

"Me too!" Carol chimed in.

"Now we're moving forward," Laura said. "We'll be here for two days and then we're going to Rome. The three of us have decided to take the Giotti family icon back to Italy, where it had been passed from generation to generation for more than three hundred years. Eduardo shouldn't have given it to me. First of all, he wasn't even the oldest son. The family was pretty upset about that, especially when I took the icon with me back to the States. When I left, I didn't know the whole story and was happy to have such a beautiful reminder of my romantic summer in Rome."

Melissa continued her mother's story. "We'll give the icon to Eduardo's older brother so he can give it to his grandson. We've talked to Antonio, and the whole family is excited about meeting us. Eduardo never married again, and didn't have any other children, so they're anxious to meet me, his only daughter. As you can imagine, we're anxious to meet his family, especially his mother—my grandmother and Carol's great-grandmother. I never got to meet my birth father, but at least I can help grant one of his last wishes, and that's going to be good for me."

Everyone at the table smiled as Carol said again, "Me too!"

Epilogue

Here we leave the Tuesday Table Ladies and the Oakwood Retirement Community to their pastimes in peaceful surroundings. But something has changed. The women know that without their persistent intervention, a valuable icon would never have found its way to its proper destiny. Laura and her family would not have found a new family in Italy, and Eduardo's death would have been in vain. And Carol might never have had the thrill of driving a classic racing green Jaguar.

The Tuesday Table Ladies have discovered that there is indeed "many a good tune to be played on old fiddles." What will they be up to next?

About the Authors

O ctavia Long is the pseudonym for eight women who dine together every Tuesday at Longwood at Oakmont, a community of retirees in western Pennsylvania.

One evening, one of them failed to appear for dinner. "Where's Muriel? Could something have happened to her?" After a search, she was found. That was the inspiration for the idea of a mystery entitled *Where's Laura?* written by the Tuesday Table Ladies.

We hope you enjoyed reading it as much as we enjoyed writing it. It would not have been possible without the wizardry of the computer and the following commandments.

1. All the authors have equal partnership in this project; none has any ownership of words, characters, or ideas.

2. This means there should be no hurt feelings when one's magnificent prose is edited or deleted.

3. This collaboration will stop only when it ceases being fun.

THE TUESDAY TABLE LADIES

Dorothy B. Armistead

Doreen E. Boyce

Nancy P. Courtney

Anne K. Ducanis

Constance T. Fischer

Margaret L. Groninger

Jane L. Reimers

Muriel U. Weeks